THE FORGOTTEN DAUGHTER

THE LOST DAUGHTERS TRILOGY BOOK ONE

VIOLA TEMPEST

The Forgotten Daughter
The Lost Daughters Trilogy Book One

Website: www.violatempest.com

Cover Design by Ann Fleur Art

The Forgotten Daughter

THE LOST DAUGHTERS TRILOGY BOOK ONE

VIOLA TEMPEST

KINGDOM OF PEACE
BAOSHU KINGDOM
HEPIN
SHENHUA KINGDOM

ORPHANAGE
N
W
E
S
JINU KINGDOM
NAJAE ISLAND

CONTENTS

CHAPTER ONE

SHE FELL INTO SYNC WITH THE SKY, HER EYES FOLLOWING THE speeding birds, her nostrils inhaling the moist air with every breath. It was another ordinary day in the leaden winters of the kingdom of Heping, China, also known as the "Kingdom of Peace."

With her gaze shifted from the sky to the cluttered town, Xiuying looked over the small town of the colossal kingdom—its tiny homes, the busy streets, and wandering people—from the tall castle towers, thinking to herself, "Where did it all go wrong?"

Standing on the grand terrace, witnessing a spectacular sunset, and seized by an acute sense of loneliness, she held a letter in her hand from her parents, remembering all the torturous memories of her past.

"After twenty years?" she asked herself with confusion. "Why now?"

Heping, China was divided into different kingdoms, ruled by the most powerful and wealthiest tribal families. Xiuying was born in the magical kingdom of Jinu, a kingdom unlike any other. It was surrounded by mountains, lakes, and trees, a scenic masterpiece, and people from all around the world would visit to see the eye-catching views for themselves.

The rulers of Jinu were the royal family, who had magical powers that controlled the sun and the moon, the ability to turn light into dark and dark into light. Because of this, they were respected by some and feared by many.

The king, Qianfan, was known for his bravery and brutal honesty. He was a tall, strong, and muscular man with sharp hazel-shaped eyes and short dark black hair. He was unforgiving, and he believed in punishing those who stepped out of bounds. Still, he was respected by his people, and for the most part, everyone obeyed his laws.

Qianfan was a strong ruler, and he made several beneficial decisions for his kingdom that led to prosperity. But as vigorous as he was, he had a soft spot for one person, one woman... his wife. Daiyu, with hair that fell down to her knees, rosy cheeks, and large eyes on a petite face. She was the most beautiful of all the queens in all the kingdoms and adored by all the kings.

In fact, Qianfan was often infatuated by her that he'd let her run his kingdom, though, the people of Jinu never minded. Daiyu had the kindest soul and a big heart.

Less than a year after they tied the knot, they decided to have a child and start a family.

However, during this time, the one child rule was still in place. This rule had been established during the last decade to prevent the increasing population. However, the rule was rejected by several kingdoms, but it led to the creation of norms that were going to leave a scar on many souls. Because of the rule, the families who still abided by it preferred to have sons over daughters so they could carry on their legacy, and having a daughter instead meant great shame for the family.

Qianfan wanted a son more than anything else. In fact, even *he* believed that Daiyu was carrying a boy because he knew he was too powerful and great of a man to breed something that would dishonor his name and kingdom. And whenever he spoke with Daiyu about the child, he'd always address the child as a *him* or a *he*, the security in his tone scaring Daiyu and making her anxious.

"What if it's a girl?" she'd ask cautiously.

"That won't happen, my love," Qianfan replied. "It *has* to be a boy; it just has to."

He'd then smile, kiss her on the forehead, and leave the room, not even waiting for her to reply. He didn't want to hear anything else she had to say about the matter; Qianfan wanted what he wanted.

The celebrations in the kingdom started months before the child was born, the castle receiving ample gifts and goods for the child. And this was all beginning to worry Daiyu. Everyone expected her to have a boy, and she started to worry about what would happen if that wasn't the case.

"What if I have a daughter?" Daiyu whispered quietly to Mei, her trusted maid and soon-to-be nanny of the child.

Mei was an incredible listener and Daiyu's only friend in the entire kingdom. She'd listen to the queen's concerns, her problems, and would give her advice whenever Daiyu needed it. Mei was in her early thirties, petite, with fair skin and shoulder-length hair. The queen always adored her and her presence.

"What do you mean, Daiyu?" Mei asked hesitantly. "Qianfan seems certain that the child is a boy."

"But what if it's not? I fear his reaction, and I fear what he will do to me and the child if he finds out."

"Oh, Daiyu. You're being silly. You know how much Qianfan loves you, and he's going to love the child as well, no matter what the gender might be. Sure, he's excited about having a boy, but he'll love a girl just the same. Trust me." She then walked over to Daiyu. "My dear, don't worry. Everything will be okay," Mei told Daiyu with a smile.

Daiyu sighed, hoping that Mei was right, but these words only brought her temporary comfort.

"I guess you're right," Daiyu said instead of what she was really thinking, that Mei didn't know what she was talking about, and Qianfan would kill her if a daughter popped out instead of a son. "Thank you."

As the months flew by, Daiyu continued to worry about the outcomes of giving birth to a daughter. What was coming ahead was uncertain, but something she would never have imagined would happen to her.

Eight and a half months in, Daiyu started experiencing labor pains. Mei rushed to call her doctor, and Qianfan joined her side as soon as he could, prepared for the premature birth of his firstborn son. And after six long hours of labor, Daiyu's screams awakening the entire kingdom and splitting Qianfan's ears, they finally heard a cry, the cry of a perfectly healthy little... girl.

Daiyu smiled when the doctor handed the child to her, her grin quickly fading away when she saw the baby's face. She looked over at Qianfan, who looked like he was ready to faint, or explode, whichever came first.

"This is *not* possible. My firstborn *cannot* be a daughter!" he yelled at the top of his lungs as his eyes grew red with anger.

He slammed the door shut as he left Daiyu's room, and ordered Mei and the doctor *not* to share the news of the child's birth to *anyone*. He then left the castle, Daiyu passing out on her pillow from the pain. But even in her dream, she couldn't help but wonder what the consequences would be for her... what the consequences would be for her daughter.

Hours later, Daiyu woke up. She was delighted to see the little girl by her side, and she held her in her arms.

"Where is Qianfan?" Daiyu asked Mei with a smile.

Mei shrugged, and as soon as Daiyu saw her face turn numb, she immediately knew that Qianfan was still upset.

"It's okay. I can go talk to him. He'll be able to accept our daughter because she's just like me," Daiyu tried to assure her friend.

However, while Daiyu was asleep, Qianfan did the unthinkable, and he told the people of his kingdom that the child had not survived the birth, that Daiyu had a miscarriage.

"This is a dark, dark day for us and for our kingdom. We are deeply saddened and would appreciate it if we were given some time to mourn. The funeral will be held tomorrow," Qianfan stated.

When he returned inside, he found Daiyu waiting for him. He still loved his wife, but he couldn't stand to look at the child. He refused to believe that *it* was his.

"But she's your daughter, Qianfan. She's just like me," Daiyu pleaded with teary eyes.

"No, she's not, and nobody can ever know of her. She is to remain unidentified and confined within the walls of this castle. This *disgrace* is not my daughter, and I do not accept her as my firstborn." Qianfan fumed with rage. "We are going to hold a funeral tomorrow to honor the miscarriage that I've told everyone you had."

Daiyu couldn't believe what she had just heard; it was almost as if the news of his daughter's birth fell on deaf ears. Qianfan ordered Mei to keep the child in her custody, and she agreed, taking the child away from Daiyu on the first day of her being a mother. Mei hated that she had to be the one to hurt the queen, her friend, like this, but she had no other choice.

Daiyu was distressed, but at ease with the fact that the child was with someone she trusted. The horrible night slowly passed away, and soon, the sun rose over the horizon. Daiyu couldn't sleep all night, though Qianfan slept like a baby, knowing that he had protected his reputation and honor.

He woke up and hugged his wife. "Forget about it, Daiyu. This never happened."

But she was stunned to see how cold-hearted Qianfan was about his own child. "What do you mean? How can you—how can *we*—forget an entire existence?"

"She's not welcomed or accepted, and it's better for you, for us, that you forget about her," Qianfan answered in a calm tone as she pushed him away.

"No! She's our daughter; we have to mark her with

the stone, Qianfan. She's one of us, please!" Daiyu sobbed and fell to the floor.

The magical stone was kept safe and a secret in the kingdom, a stone used to engrave the symbol of their tribe onto the child's hand, giving them their magical power. It allowed them to control the light and the dark. They could use the light to grow plants and trees, or turn day into night whenever they wanted.

Each family member had a symbol engraved on their hand since birth. It was that symbol that gave them these abilities.

Qianfan begrudgingly picked up the child and said, "Alright, Daiyu, I'm going to mark her with the stone, but after that, you have to promise me that you are going to make yourself forget about this *abomination.*"

Daiyu looked up at him with teary eyes, and then nodded her head in agreement. She knew he was never going to come around; he was *never* going to accept her. But at least their daughter would have her power.

Before the funeral, Qianfan and Daiyu went to go see their daughter. Daiyu took the girl in her arms and cried as she carried her toward the room where the stone was kept.

Qianfan recited the enchanting words, "From blood to blood and the bond it creates, mark what differentiates us from the rest of the mates," and placed the stone on his daughter's wrist.

The stone glowed and made its mark.

"Oh, my daughter. We're going to call you *Xiuying.*

And no matter what anyone else says, you represent the kingdom of Jinu, and you are a precious gem," Daiyu whispered in her tiny ear.

Then, with a heavy heart, she handed Xiuying over to Mei, and Qianfan pulled his wife out of the room.

"I hope you keep your word, Daiyu, just like I kept mine," he told her, to which she nodded with a crest-fallen face.

As she stood beside Qianfan at the funeral, Daiyu realized that her family was forever going to be a jigsaw puzzle that never seemed to fit together.

"How does it feel having a funeral for someone who's still alive?" Daiyu whispered to Qianfan in the saddest tone he had ever heard.

"I don't feel anything because there's nothing to be upset about," he replied with a smirk.

"Maybe the funeral is for us, then. For our dead hearts, Qianfan," Daiyu remarked sarcastically.

Qianfan stayed silent. Her words stung, but he still loved her, more than he loved anything else. Although his patience was quickly fading, he tried not to talk back as he feared hurting her even more.

The castle was full of townspeople coming in to comfort the king and queen. They brought white flowers and dried fruits to offer their condolences. Qianfan could see that Daiyu was exhausted, and he told her to go get some rest. She nodded and walked toward her room.

She tried and tried, but she couldn't sleep, the daughter whom she had to forget eating her alive.

"She will always feel incomplete and abandoned," she heard herself say. Her thoughts continued to cloud her mind as she heard a knock on the door. "Come i-in," she stuttered, and the door opened.

It was Mei. Daiyu couldn't contain her emotions and started to cry.

"Mei, I gave birth to a daughter, and people are acting like I'd lost a child. Is it really that awful to let them know that I have a healthy baby girl?"

"Oh, Daiyu, it's not. Your daughter is a beautiful little girl, and she's right here inside the castle, under my care. I promise you that she's going to be well-loved and cared for. Stop letting your thoughts take control of you. It's not your fault. You fought for her, and that's what a mother does. Don't be so hard on yourself. I'm sorry that you were the one who had to suffer, Daiyu, but the rules of society were put in place to protect the honor of the kingdom." Mei tried to comfort her as Daiyu sat on the white marble floor and cried her heart out.

"From now on, no more tears, my queen," Mei said politely, and Daiyu nodded.

When the funeral ended, Qianfan entered the room and found Daiyu sitting on the floor. She was asleep, and for a moment, Qianfan felt regret. Because of his decision, Daiyu had fallen into great depression.

"Daiyu, wake up."

Daiyu opened her eyes, but she was too weak to get up, so Qianfan carried her to their bed. He started to talk about how the kings from other kingdoms had written to him, expressing their condolences, but she refrained from indulging in the conversation and remained quiet.

After a few moments of silence, Qianfan whispered, "I will always love you, Daiyu."

"But not more than your honor," she retorted.

Qianfan felt another sting to his heart, but walked away instead of saying anything back.

The day soon turned to night, and Qianfan started to question himself. He understood that Daiyu was *never* going to see him in the same light again. He knew that their relationship would change drastically. And he could only blame Xiuying for it.

"I wish you'd died, Xiuying," he whispered to himself. "You're the reason why Daiyu hates me, and I'll *never* forgive you for that."

BABY XIUYING WAS COMPLETELY OBLIVIOUS TO WHAT WAS going on, or how her life was going to end up. She was unaware of the fact that her mother never wanted to give her away; she was unaware that her father hated her. She was unaware that the woman who was looking after her was only her nanny, and not her mother.

Xiuying was an adorable child with a chubby face and bright smile. All the nannies inside the castle adored her, and they loved making her giggle. Mei stayed with her the most, but because of her other responsibilities inside the castle, she had to appoint different nannies for Xiuying.

And even though Qianfan didn't accept her as his firstborn, and despite the hatred he had for her, he instructed that the staff take great care of her as so to keep Daiyu satisfied. The best cuisines, fruits, and clothes were given to her, and her innocence to her surroundings kept her happy.

However, Daiyu could see and hear everything that was happening around her. Her heart died every day, seeing her daughter being carried by one nanny after another. The burden of abandoning her child was too heavy on her. And the distance between Qianfan and Daiyu began increasing with every second, despite the attempts of Qianfan to make amends. What he did could not be fixed, and they both knew it. One blamed the other while the other blamed the child.

Days and nights passed, the seasons changing from winter to spring, from summer to autumn, and soon enough, six years had gone by. And though the marriage that had been hanging by a thread had become a little more robust over the years, things were never the same as they were before Xiuying was born.

Qianfan was still in love with Daiyu, and Daiyu was still trying to accept what had happened, but still numb.

Qianfan's mother, Qiang, had also come to stay with them. She was a petite and elderly woman, had a thin, wrinkled face, graying hair, and a terrible temper. Like her son, she, too, hated Xiuying because she felt like all the happiness had been stolen from the castle the day Xiuying was born.

And Xiuying, now six years old, was beginning to look more and more like her mother. She was taught at the castle by one of her nannies, intelligent and a quick learner. She'd even learned how to read and write proficiently by the age of four. However, she had no friends her own age, and she only ever interacted with Mei and the other nannies.

Mei and Xiuying were close; it almost felt like they were mother and daughter. Xiuying would come to her if she needed help with anything, and Mei would always comfort her, console her, just like she did with Daiyu. But still, Xiuying knew from a very young age who her true parents were. Daiyu begged her friend to let her daughter know, but to also tell Xiuying to never contact them, reach out to them, or even speak about them. Her parents lived on the other side of the castle, and Xiuying never saw them face-to-face. It was hard for her, knowing that her parents didn't want to be near her, but she still felt safe with Mei by her side.

Luckily, she was still too young to understand what this all meant, why this was happening. What she *did* know was that, whatever the reason was, it involved a lot of hate. She could sense the rage that her father had for her, and would often find herself questioning whether she had ever been loved, loneliness and sadness shivering in her soul.

She didn't hate her parents; she didn't know them enough to do so, but she still had questions that needed answers. Xiuying was much brighter than the other children her age. She could understand things that even adults could not comprehend, but she was awkward around new people and got anxious often.

Daiyu kept an eye on her daughter during the first few years of her life, asking Mei to bring her out into the yard to play so Daiyu could see her from through her window. She'd pretend that she was talking to Xiuying, tears flowing from her eyes when she realized that she wasn't, though Xiuying had been too young to remember. But eventually, she stopped, choosing her husband over the little girl.

Xiuying knew that she canopied under the mantle of secrecy and silence in the castle, and made peace with it at a very young age. Ever since Qiang came to stay, she was determined to ruin Xiuying's peace. Qiang moved closer to Xiuying's room in order to keep an eye on her, and she took every chance she could to insult her.

"She's an abomination! Ruining both my son and his kingdom. What would the people think if they were to ever find out?" Xiuying would often hear Qiang say from down the hall.

And she continued every chance she got, making sure the girl knew that she wasn't wanted.

"You're bad luck for our family. That's why your parents left you," Qiang told Xiuying once.

It shattered her, her reflection a constant reminder that she was a flaw and a burden to her own family. Qiang made Xiuying believe that she was unloved, and

Xiuying believed it as the truth. She knew that her mother was never going to change her mind and suddenly love her again, and this made her hyper-aware of all her flaws, feeling foreign in her own body, and like she didn't even belong in her own skin. Growing up, Xiuying had put Daiyu high up on a pedestal, something she was beginning to regret.

"I don't understand why she doesn't want me. Why they just abandoned me, forgot about me," she'd say to Mei while pacing back and forth.

Mei could see that her anxious thoughts had started to take over her, all these questions with no answers.

"Xiuying, I want you to do something for me, okay?" Mei said one day.

"What is it, Mei?" Xiuying asked politely.

"Every time you feel like your heart is heavy, or you feel anxious, I want you to close your eyes and think about a place where you feel calm, comfortable, and happy. It may be the beach, a forest, your bedroom, somewhere else. Imagine what this place looks like, sounds like, and imagine how good you feel when you're there. Try it; take a deep breath."

Xiuying closed her eyes, and she soon found herself out in the yard. She could hear the sound of the wind, feel the cold breeze, and smell the fragrance of the jasmine flowers planted nearby. Most importantly, she felt like her mother was watching her. She believed that she was seen, and that, was her happy place.

As soon as she opened her eyes, she realized that she felt much calmer. She saw Mei smiling in front of her and gave her a hug.

"Thank you, Mei," Xiuying whispered.

"Promise me that you'll do this every time you feel down, my child."

"I promise," she replied.

"I know, Xiuying, that this must be very hard for you to understand, but you need to know that you cannot control what other people say, and you cannot let their words get to you. Other people are other people, and you are you. The only words that should matter must be your own, and yours alone. You will be punishing yourself if you keep letting these harsh words get to you; you have to learn to let them go," Mei calmly said, and Xiuying nodded.

After this heartfelt conversation, Mei and Xiuying went into the kitchen and enjoyed their favorite dessert, red bean cake, like they always did. Daiyu hardly ever checked up on Xiuying, and Mei was surprised to see how Daiyu had moved on with her life, leaving Xiuying behind. Daiyu started getting caught up in her own life, going to social gatherings and taking up social welfare projects to keep herself occupied. It was obvious that she was running away from her feelings, but she was leaving a lot behind, and Mei feared that it'd be too late when she'd finally realize.

Mei hardly ever saw Daiyu anymore, and their friendship drifted apart with time.

However, while Mei had all these feelings, Daiyu was jealous, jealous that Xiuying was close to her and was getting closer to her day by day. She would often think that Mei took her place, took her daughter from her. She tried to remain modest; she tried to be understanding, but she envied the motherly bond that Mei had with Xiuying.

"At least Xiuying has a motherly figure in her life," she said to herself and decided to maintain distance.

She started to avoid Mei for the sake of her daughter, never wanting her jealousy to get in the way of the beautiful relationship that Mei and Xiuying had formed. But what Daiyu didn't realize was that, even though Xiuying had Mei by her side, she still craved for her mother's love, her mother's presence.

After all, her happy place was in front of her mother's eyes.

CHAPTER TWO

QIANFAN'S HATE FOR XIUYING DID NOT LESSEN OVER TIME. He tolerated her but could not accept her. He didn't care that he was missing his daughter's early years, or that his decision was affecting more than just himself. It was almost as if Xiuying didn't exist for him. Like he had forgotten about her.

It was another monotonous day at the castle, where Xiuying remained a trapped princess. She had a young soul and was determined to find silver linings in her life. She made herself believe that every day was a new day to learn from, to fix mistakes, and move forward.

She sat in her room, learning how to paint. Mei had given her some paints and several canvases. Xiuying always had a habit of painting the secret garden of the castle; it was her happy place, and nobody else visited it. The only thing she hated about it was that she had to walk past Qiang's room to get to the garden, and Qiang *always* had eyes on her.

Most of the time, Xiuying would only go into the garden when Qiang was away, but whenever Qiang noticed where she was going, she'd follow her, make sure she wasn't up to anything. There was a dark room at the end of the hallway, where they stored armors and old statues. Xiuying was not fond of that room. It always gave her chills, shivers throughout her body, whenever she looked inside it, her imagination making her think that the room had ghostly spirits inside it.

It was late afternoon, dark black clouds over the castle, and winds blowing hard against the trees, dark yet beautiful, and Xiuying decided that she wanted to paint out in the garden.

"It seems like a good day to paint, right?" Xiuying asked Mei.

"I think not. It's about to rain," she answered.

"I'll be back before it rains, Mei. I promise!" Xiuying answered and ran off with her paints, brushes, and a tiny canvas.

On her way to the garden, she passed by Qiang's

bedroom door and felt relieved when she found her sleeping. She tiptoed her way through the hallway and reached the dark room. She always peeked through the windows but never stepped foot inside. But this time, something inside her told her to go in.

"Why not? Life is about trying new things, right?" she asked herself, opened the door, and entered.

There was dust everywhere. The armors were covered with a white cloth that almost looked like they were possessed. She looked around and found a statue of her mother and father with a baby in her mother's hands. Xiuying walked closer and brushed the layers of dust off of them. It was dark, and the windows were slamming shut because of the wind, when suddenly, she heard a shrieking voice with the anger of a thousand dragons.

"It was *never* supposed to be you!"

Xiuying looked back in fear and realized that Qiang was standing at the door. Xiuying couldn't see her face, but she could see a black shadowy figure. As soon as Xiuying realized what was happening, Qiang closed the room's doors and locked her inside. Xiuying ran toward the doors and shouted at the top of her lungs.

"Grandmother! Qiang! Please, let me out; let me out! I'm scared of the dark, please!"

She continued to bang against the door, but Qiang ignored her pleas and cries. With an evil grin, she walked toward her own room and closed her bedroom door.

Meanwhile, little Xiuying was all alone. All she could see were white sheets covering armors, and a statue that she could not understand. It was dark, and getting darker as each minute passed. Xiuying couldn't help but cry, her body starting to shiver, and tears rolling down her cheeks.

"Mother, please, come save me! I need you," she screamed out loud.

The silence in the room forced her words to invade her mind. As a six-year-old, it was difficult for her to snap out of her own thoughts.

You are bad luck; you're not supposed to be here. The words echoed and whispered to her again and again. The voices were overlapping, and it almost felt like she was inside a well, and the harsh words were surrounding her.

Xiuying closed her eyes and tried to imagine her happy place, but she couldn't do it.

"My happy place cannot be someone who abandoned me." Her eyes were red and swollen as she stood up and walked toward the statue of her parents. "You are *nothing* to me anymore. You abandoned me, and I hate you and will *never* forgive you."

She shrugged as shivers traveled her spine. Before this, she had never hated her parents. She'd always hope that maybe the decision made by her parents had a valid reason and that maybe, only maybe, one day, they would take her back with love and open arms. However, the darkness inside the room had taken away the last tiny ray of sunshine that Xiuying had left in her heart.

Many hours passed, the thunder roared, and the room that Xiuying was trapped inside started to grow colder. When Mei realized that Xiuying was nowhere to be found, she checked everywhere, in her room, in the other nannies' rooms, out in the yard, in the kitchen. Nothing. There was no sign of her, and panic started to take over Mei's heart.

Soon, word spread like wildfire across the staff, and everyone started to look for Xiuying. Qiang stayed silent, watching everyone freak out and worry as if it were her own comedy show. The guards were looking for her, the maids were looking for her, the nannies were looking for her, and Mei was going crazy, running from one end of the castle to the other. The dullness of the night had taken over as the clock struck midnight, and there was *still* no sign of Xiuying.

Xiuying had fallen asleep for several hours before she awoken again, wondering if anyone had even noticed that she was missing. The questions that were popping up in her own mind made her cry, yet once again, but this time, with all her will and rage, she started to bang against the doors. Lucky for her, Mei was close by, and she ran to the direction where the faint noise was coming from... and found herself in Qiang's hallway.

The room that Xiuying was trapped in was in the corner of a dark alley. Mei rushed toward the doors and swung them open, and Xiuying quickly rushed outside.

"Oh, sweetheart, we have been looking for you for hours! I was worried sick. Don't ever scare me like that again." Mei pulled Xiuying into a warm hug. Xiuying's body was cold, and she was shivering with fear. "It's okay, Xiuying. I'm here," Mei told her, but Xiuying remained quiet.

Mei had showed up for her; that's what mothers do. And her own mother was clueless that her own child had gone missing this entire time. Xiuying started to realize that it was time to say goodbye to all the hopes she had for her parents.

She used to make excuses for them, but no more. It was time to move on.

As she broke free from Mei's grasp, Xiuying said, "Thank you, Mei."

"No matter where you are, where you go, I will *always* come find you, Xiuying. I will *always* look out for you," Mei replied.

LATER THAT NIGHT, MEI STAYED BY XIUYING'S SIDE AFTER she had tucked her into bed, and started to suspect that Qiang had been the cause of the little girl getting trapped inside that room.

"I'm sorry, my child. You don't deserve all this pain that you're experiencing. I wish I could do something, but there's not much in my control," she whispered to Xiuying as the child fell asleep.

Mei decided that she was going to go talk to Daiyu because the actions of Qiang were getting out of hand, and they were affecting Xiuying's well-being.

The next day, Mei went to the queen's room. Daiyu had changed a lot of things. Her room had a different color scheme, changing from pastels to darker shades. The paintings of natural sceneries were removed and replaced by faux animal heads. The room was lit up with candles, and the drapes were down even though it was the middle of the day.

It almost feels like all the joy has left her life, Mei thought as she knocked on the door.

"Come in, come in, whoever it is," Daiyu said in a cheerful tone, and after hearing her voice, Mei started to second guess herself. Daiyu *did* sound happy, or was it all fake?

"Oh! It's you. It's been so long. So happy to see you again!" Daiyu exclaimed with a grin.

"I'm glad to see you, too. There's actually something that I need to talk to you about," Mei replied.

"What is it?" Daiyu asked in a curious and slightly irritated manner.

"It's Xiuying, your daughter," Mei answered and told her what had happened last night.

However, Daiyu didn't respond like Mei had thought she would. "So, what? Are you accusing the king's mother of something so wicked?"

Mei stood silent.

"You do *not* question royalty, Mei. You are nothing but a mere maid, a servant. You do *not* question what's above and beyond your entire existence. I will suggest that you take these nonsensical thoughts of yours somewhere else. The girl is *your* responsibility. You must protect her. If that is something you cannot do, stop making excuses for it," Daiyu said as her tone grew harsher.

Mei felt devastated over the response that she had gotten from the queen, from her friend. "Yes, my queen. I shall obey," she responded and left the room with a heavy heart.

What had happened to Daiyu was beyond Mei's understanding, but after the conversation, Mei promised herself that she'd never go to Daiyu for anything ever again.

On the other hand, Daiyu was regretful for what her daughter was going through, for how she had spoken to Mei. She felt confused, about herself and about everything around her. After their conversation, she sat down in front of the window, feeling something that she couldn't explain with words, and wrote in her journal what was beyond her understanding.

We all have someone we don't speak about, someone who is everything to us, but the world keeps us apart. Xiuying's presence, her name churns my stomach, and the remembrance of her scent from when I held her for the first time is still fresh. Xiuying is someone I can never stop loving, even if I cannot have her in my life. Forgetting about her is an impossible task.

Her marriage with Qianfan was finally getting back on track after the chaos that had ensued when her daughter was born. It was his orders to forget about her daughter, and at this point, she only knew one thing.

"You do not question the king, especially when it is someone like Qianfan," she whispered to herself.

DAYS PASSED SINCE THE INCIDENT HAD HAPPENED, AND Xiuying found herself struggling trying to return to normal. She started to grow afraid of the dark even more, sleeping with the room lit bright. Most of the time, in the middle of the night, she would wake up with fear and scream. She also found herself beginning to speak with a stutter, and she complained of hallucinations that Qiang was always around her, always near her, whispering words of hatred into her ears.

Mei, and everyone in the castle who interacted with Xiuying, noticed how differently she was behaving after the incident, and they all worried for her.

One evening during supper, Mei and Xiuying had one of their heartfelt conversations.

"Xiuying, you have to move on, my dear. I know it's hard, but you need to love yourself. I understand that, at this point, the most difficult form of love for you is self-love. You have always given more than you have received, and that is exhausting, I'm sure. You're worth every fight; you're worth this life. Laugh a little, get back to things that bring joy to you. Get rid of the loose ends that make you feel unseen."

Xiuying heard her, shook her head, and stated, "But how do I do that?"

"Xiuying, maybe you should write a letter about your feelings. I know it's hard for you to speak up to me or to anyone, and that is fine, but keeping your feelings to yourself will only haunt you. You have to let them out, or else they are going to affect you in ways you would not understand," Mei suggested.

Xiuying smiled, took a sip of her tea, and replied, "You always have such insightful suggestions, Mei. Maybe I will write a letter, but who do I write the letter to?"

"You can address it to anyone you want. Just write whatever you feel, whatever you are experiencing, and hide it somewhere. Nobody has to read it if you don't want them to," Mei answered politely.

That evening soon ended, and the darkness of the night started to take control while Xiuying was getting ready for bed. Mei tucked the girl into bed, kissed her goodnight, and left the room. Xiuying tried to close her eyes but could not get herself to fall asleep. All of her thoughts and memories were rushing into her mind, when finally, she decided that she was going to write them all down. She hopped out of bed, went over to her desk, and looked for a quill and ink.

"Where is it? Where is it?" she kept mumbling to herself. "Ah, finally."

She grabbed the items and a sheet of paper. This was the first time she had felt excited about doing something after the unfortunate event. She sat down on her desk and began to write.

Dear Friend,

I have been holding onto something that I need to let go of. It's something that no longer exists, but I still think about it all the time. I have been holding onto family that were not mine from the very beginning. I kept them safe in my heart because I was scared to give up on them and the hopes of being together one day. But a recent event made me realize that it's time to move on, that I don't need them anymore. That all I need is myself.

So, I am writing to let go.

I am writing to move on.

Yours truly,

X

She didn't sign her name because she didn't want to, but she felt much better after writing the letter. She folded the sheet of paper and placed it inside a scroll.

"Mei was right; this does help," she told herself and smiled. "Mei is always right."

THE NEXT DAY, XIUYING WOKE UP AND WENT OUT TO THE cherry blossom tree that she could see from her window, and she tied the scroll onto a branch, hiding the letter in the tree. However, when she woke up the day after, she noticed that her scroll was gone, and there was another one in its place. Confused, she ran out toward the tree. She was right. There *was* another scroll. Someone had replied to her letter! She took the scroll down and rushed toward her room. Unable to maintain her excitement, she sat at her desk and opened it.

To the little girl with the strongest soul,

Sometimes we have to go through these tough times and learn what is and isn't right for us. And that is the most valuable thing we can learn in life because that is how we get to know about the people and things that are meant to be with us. So, always remember that letting go is a part of your journey, even if you have to go back and go down a different road. Letting go will take you to places you never knew you wanted to go.

Keep your head up high.

Yours faithfully,

A Well-Wisher

Xiuying was in awe while reading the letter. She couldn't believe that someone had *actually* answered her! And with such wisdom, too. The words touched her heart, and she believed in them, a pinch of hope for her future in this bewildering castle. But then she paused.

"What if it's Mei?" she asked herself and started to march toward Mei's room, where she was nowhere to be found. "Hm, where could she be?"

She then walked into the kitchen and found Mei making her favorite dessert, red bean cake with straw-berries. The fragrance of the sweet sugar wafted throughout the room and almost distracted Xiuying from what she'd wanted to say.

"Hi, there, my dear. What a surprise seeing you down here!" Mei exclaimed, noticing that Xiuying's mood had suddenly shifted from crestfallen to joyful.

"So, remember how you told me to write a letter about my feelings?" Xiuying started, and Mei nodded. "Well, I wrote one and hid it somewhere, but apparently, someone found it and replied to it."

"What do you mean?" Mei asked, confused.

"I got another letter in the place where I had hidden mine. I thought it was you!" Xiuying said in suspicion.

"I certainly did not," Mei replied with a firm face, and then laughed. "You really think it was me? That's funny!"

"Mei, are you sure it wasn't you?" Xiuying asked again.

Mei knelt down, tucked a strand of the child's hair behind her ear, and whispered, "Yes, my dear. I am positive that it wasn't me. Trust me."

Xiuying still had her doubts, but she believed Mei. Now, the new mystery was this new person with such beautiful insights. Xiuying was now more determined than ever to find out who it was, because the person who wrote the letter clearly knew much about her. She needed to find out more, so she decided to write another one.

Dear Friend,

I'm surprised that you replied to a letter that no one was supposed to read, but I am genuinely grateful for the heartfelt response that you had written. You made me feel happy again, and it was something I had thought I lost. Since you know who I am, judging by your last letter, it would be fair for me to know your identity as well. After all, we are friends, right?

Yours truly,

X

Xiuying signed the letter with another X, tied it to the same spot on the tree, and waited eagerly for a response.

She woke up the next day, and there it was!

To the little girl filled with curiosity,

I will not reveal who I am because I wish to remain a secret. I cannot help but notice what you wrote about happiness. You must understand that happiness comes when we are listening to the words of another, or are noticing the beauty of the world around us. You've read and heard my words; hence, you felt the true joy of happiness. But remember, do not associate your happiness with someone else's presence because happiness comes from within.

Yours faithfully,

A Well-Wisher

Xiuying felt overwhelmed by the amount of extraordinary wisdom this person had. She was surprised that she understood what was written, but what bothered her was the wish to stay a secret.

"Why would this person not want me to know

about them?" she asked Mei one night while heading to bed.

"Maybe it is for your own good, Xiuying. Don't think about this too much. Whoever this is, is a kindred spirit."

CHAPTER THREE

WHILE XIUYING WAS STRUGGLING TO FIGURE OUT WHO THIS mysterious person was, Daiyu and Qianfan received exciting news. They were expecting another child! After six years, the queen was pregnant again, something the people in their kingdom began to spread around very quickly. Soon, presents from all around the kingdom started to come into the castle, congratulating the king and queen.

Daiyu was caught by surprise because she had not planned for this, and it was already three months into her pregnancy. The thought of having another child scared her, especially since she already had Xiuying.

The presents, the praise, the celebration, it all made her feel like the past was coming back to haunt her, from which she had tried to run from for a very long time. Qianfan, over time, had become even more of a pessimist, yet still proud because of all his achievements in the betterment of the kingdom. His entitlement had grown and overshadowed every meaningful relationship he had in his life.

Times had changed, but Qianfan had not. He was still expecting a son and calling the child a firstborn in front of other people. Daiyu felt lost, and the only person she wanted to talk to was Mei, whom she had pushed away. Ever since Daiyu heard the news of her new child, she had grown quieter. Qianfan noticed, and he tried his best to bring her everything she liked in an attempt to cheer her up, to provide her with the best of the best.

He'd work less to spend more time with her, but that wasn't what she needed. What she needed was the surety that she would *actually* get a chance at motherhood this time, no matter what the gender turned out to be. But Qianfan was so certain that it would be a son, just like last time. He addressed the child as a *he*, even in front of his wife, and he wanted what he wanted. He wasn't going to compromise at any cost, but this situation felt like a living nightmare to Daiyu.

History was repeating itself, and she had gotten no

closure from what'd happened before. There were questions, and only questions, lingering in her mind.

Why me? I have given up so much, compromised so much for our marriage, that all I have left is emptiness. I've loved, lost, and Qianfan just doesn't seem to care. I wonder about the past; I look for closure, but there's none. The truth is, I'm still holding onto these unknown answers, so much that I've started to obsess over what could've been. She wrote to herself as she felt emotionally exhausted.

Celebration was in the air as months passed by, and the child was about to come into this world. Every day at the castle, new gifts were coming for the child, and it was happening right in front of Xiuying's eyes. The more she tried to ignore the festivities, the more they were prominently in front of her.

Mei was given the responsibility of hosting a dinner for some of the royal families who were coming to congratulate the king and queen. This kept Mei occupied, and she hardly ever got a chance to see Xiuying. Xiuying wondered if things were just as fast-paced and celebrated right before *her* birth.

"My birth was not celebrated, but was the news of my existence celebrated?" she asked herself.

She soon felt overwhelmed by all her emotions. This child was going to be her sibling! She often wondered how that would feel, but then she'd distract herself from such thoughts because she knew that she would never be given the chance to meet him or her. She would just be isolated from her baby brother or sister, just like she was isolated from her parents.

This month was also her birth month, and she was about to turn seven. She felt old, even though she was still only a child, like she had lived a lifetime. Every year, Mei would plan a mini surprise birthday party for her, where she'd bake Xiuying's favorite red bean cake, buy her presents, and decorate her room.

Xiuying's birth, birthday, and mini parties were always kept a secret. At the same time, the rest of the castle mourned the death of Qianfan and Daiyu's first-born. Xiuying looked forward to her birthday this year because Mei would always go out of her way to celebrate it.

It was only three days away, and Xiuying was eagerly waiting. She felt like a directionless balloon in the wind with no destination in sight. She sat in her room, looking through the window, and she decided to write another letter. She'd failed to find out who the mystery writer was and hadn't written a letter in a while, so she sat down at her desk and pulled out a sheet of paper.

Dear Friend,

I know that I have not written to you in a long time, and I'm sorry for that. I haven't felt like myself lately because of all that's going on inside the castle. A life is celebrated, but not mine. Every time I try to let it go and move forward, something comes up, and all the memories start coming back. I end up wondering about many things. I wonder what birds do when they get stuck in one place. Because I feel the same way, caged. The world is lonely and sad, especially if your family chooses to abandon you; it makes you question your entire existence. I don't know why I'm here or why they chose to forget me, and that not knowing, not having answers, is what's killing me.

Tell me, is coming back to the start and beginning again the same as having never left?

Yours truly,

X

The child wrote as tears fell onto the sheet of paper. Her hands shivered as she rolled the letter and placed it inside the scroll. She threw a cloak over her body, walked toward the same cherry blossom tree, whose leaves were now beginning to fall off, and placed the scroll in the same spot.

But three days later, the day of her birthday, she didn't get a response, not like she had before. Everyone inside the castle dressed in black as they mourned for someone who was still alive while Xiuying stayed trapped inside her room, unable to let them know otherwise. And she didn't know that they were all mourning for her, that they were all mourning for her death. To protect her from the truth, Mei had told her that a noble fighter of the kingdom died on her birthday.

The entire day passed, and it was almost dark. Xiuying was eager to see what Mei had planned for her, and as the thought crossed her mind, she heard a knock on her door.

"Oh, I wonder who that could be," she said to herself and chuckled.

She opened the door, and Mei was standing there with the biggest red bean cake in her hands, along with a few bags filled with presents and decorations. Mei came in singing, placed the items on her bed, and gave the child a hug.

"Happy Birthday!" she exclaimed.

"Thank you, Mei. I love you!" Xiuying cheered, unable to contain her excitement.

They started to decorate her room with candles, balloons, streamers, and a handmade birthday banner. They lit the candles and placed the cake on her desk.

"This looks so pretty! I wish my room could look like this every day of the year!" Xiuying yelled happily.

Mei chuckled. "But that would steal the charm from it, wouldn't it?"

They both laughed, and then suddenly, the door slammed open; it was Qiang!

"Well, well, what do we have here?" Qiang remarked. "A celebration for the unwanted spawn? I see. Do you ever wonder why you have to do everything in secrecy?" She glared at Xiuying as she stepped inside.

The life from Xiuying's face vanished. Mei was furious, but she had to stay quiet for the sake of Xiuying.

"Haven't you heard? A new child is coming. A boy. And your father is just *thrilled* about his birth, unlike when you were born." Qiang blew out the candles, one after another.

"What do you mean?" Xiuying muttered.

"Oh, you naïve child. Don't you realize that you've stolen the happiness from your father? Why do you think the castle mourns on your birthday?" Qiang asked with a smile on her face. Clearly, she enjoyed every second of torturing a seven-year-old.

"Please, stop; she's just a child!" Mei hesitantly interfered, but Qiang raised her hand and indicated for her to stop.

Qiang was royalty, and Mei was just a nanny. She had no power over her.

Qiang continued, "We mourn because your father declared his first child *dead*. You are *dead* to him, yet a living weight on the shoulders of your parents. He wanted a son, but you were born instead. You brought him disappointment, and your parents drifted apart because of *you*. They both hate you, and they never want to see your face ever again. You are alive, yet everyone thinks you're dead. It would have been better if you *had* died."

Xiuying's heart sank. Her room turned dark as Qiang blew out the candles, but she finally had answers. Still, they were too heavy for her to carry. She felt scattered in the sand like strands of dried seaweed.

The silence in the room soon broke with Qiang singing, "Oh, and Happy Birthday!"

"The *audacity* of this woman knows no limits!" Mei hissed to herself as Xiuying sat feeling helpless. But she knew that Qiang was right. She couldn't help Xiuying or protect her from the truths of her life.

Xiuying was shattered, broken to such an extreme that there was nothing Mei could say to remedy that.

"Mei, can you please leave? I need some time alone," Xiuying asked her.

Mei didn't know what to say, how she could possibly console her after all that.

"Okay, I'll be in the next room if you need me," she said in such a low voice that even Xiuying could understand that Mei was feeling hopeless.

Xiuying nodded, and Mei left. The child closed the door behind her and sat down on the floor.

"What if I weren't alive anymore? Would that fix everything? Make the wrongs right?" she asked herself, the question itself so intimidating for such a young child.

She thought about what Mei would always say to her. "Your inner monologue is something that can either make or break you as a person."

But Mei wasn't here anymore, and her inner monologue was becoming more and more demeaning, pushing her to make a decision that no one thought a seven-year-old could even make.

Xiuying went outside her room and started to walk down the dark hallway. It was almost time for supper, and everyone gathered in the grand dining room, so no one saw her. She walked over to the storage room and grabbed a tiny bottle of poison that was used to kill the rats in the castle and hurried back into her room.

"What a royal way to die," she whispered to herself as she held the tiny bottle in her hands.

All of a sudden, she felt like she had grown too fast and finally understood her destiny. It was to go away for good. She wanted to write something before she left, so she sat at her desk for the last time, held her quill, and started to write.

Dear Friend,

I feel shattered. It feels like the sad days are winning, or maybe they've already declared victory. I've had times of despair and uncertainty many times before. Still, not quite like this. There is this feeling of sadness, mixed with a pinch of fear, that is creeping around inside of me. I am giving up. I have decided to go away because that is what my father wanted and my grandmother suggested. That is what I need to do to make things right.

I will always be grateful for the amount of love that Mei has shown me. She is the closest person I have to a mother, and I cherish every moment with her. She does not deserve this, but I don't deserve this, either. I hope Mei lives a happy life after I'm gone. Well-Wisher, you've brought light into my life, and I will never forget your wise words wherever I go next.

Yours truly,

X

She finished the letter and left it on her desk. Without another thought, she drank from the tiny bottle. At first, she felt fine, though a bit dizzy, so she climbed into bed. Soon, her vision started to fade away, and her eyes closed.

In the other room, Mei was worried for Xiuying. She was an adult, and even *she* couldn't stand what Qiang had said. She couldn't even begin to imagine how Xiuying had taken it. Mei couldn't fall asleep, so she decided to go and check up on the child. She knocked on the door three times, but no one answered. That was very unlikely of Xiuying, so Mei opened the door and found the little girl tucked in bed. At first, she assumed that the girl had fallen peacefully asleep, but when she stepped a little closer, she saw white liquid coming out of her mouth, and she realized that it was poison and started to scream for help!

"Someone call the doctor. Xiuying needs help!" Mei's scream was so loud that it frightened everyone inside the castle. The doctor arrived instantly and checked Xiuying's pulse. It was still there, and that meant there was hope. "Please don't leave me; please don't leave me," Mei kept repeating and prayed for a miracle while the doctor treated her.

Everyone who loved Xiuying grew devastated by the news, and they all felt sympathy for the child. While the doctor treated the girl, Mei went outside with her soul wrecked and heart stabbed. She started to reflect on everything that she could not tell Xiuying. How much she loved her, how much she wanted to be there for her, and how much she believed in her.

The news soon spread quickly, and one of the nannies rushed to inform the king and queen.

"Your daughter, Xiuying, tried to end her life," the nanny said in a panic, and Daiyu stood up, her heart dropping down to her stomach. Qianfan hated the thought of seeing his beloved wife in such distress, especially over that child again, and he felt a seething rage for his daughter.

"We have to go see her, Qianfan. I have to go see her, please!" she pleaded. "I just need to look at her once. Make sure she's okay!" And Qianfan, for once, agreed, but only because she was carrying his unborn son, and he didn't dare risk doing anything that would compromise that.

The castle halls were lit with tallow candles, and guards were standing at every corner as Qianfan and Daiyu headed toward Xiuying's room.

Mei was still in disbelief, and all she could think about was all the pain that Xiuying must have experienced to make such a crucial decision, how heartbroken she must have been, how hopeless she must have felt as these thoughts were running through her mind. Then she heard footsteps approaching down the hallway, pulling her away from her thoughts. It sounded like an army was marching toward her, and Mei looked up. Her eyes made out two shadowy figures. Tears in her eyes blurred her vision, and when she focused harder, she couldn't believe her eyes.

It was Qianfan and Daiyu! Mei felt like her heart had sunk and emerged back with vengeful rage, and before she could think to say anything else, she screamed in tears, "Now you decide to show up?! After dragging her to the depths of despair? After leaving her on her own? Look what you have done to her! This is all your fault; you have *no right* to see her, and *no right* to be with her right now. You left her and let her be, leaving her to feel abandoned her entire life just because you two are selfish!"

All eyes were on her as she fell onto her knees and started to sob. The silence in the hallway broke as Qianfan spoke in a calm, yet firm, tone. "Have you forgotten your place, Mei? Have you forgotten who you are talking to?" His tone grew stronger. "Besides, do you really think we're oblivious to what you're planning? Taking care of a child with magic and rights to our wealth, keeping her by your side, putting up a pretense to show that you actually care just so you can claim our wealth one day? You are only motivated to take care of Xiuying because of *your* personal interests." He paused, and then continued, "You crossed the line before when you questioned my mother's intentions, but this ends here. Your time ends here."

"No!" Mei shouted. "I-I will never leave her like you did. Xiuying has yearned for love ever since she was born, and I have given that to her. I played the role that you and your wife should've played. I don't want anything from you. You two are monsters, and I feel sorry for you."

She spat, her breathing heavy from the rage welling inside of her. Qianfan ordered the guards to take her away, and they did. Two guards held her from her arms and chained her hands. Her cries and screams were growing louder with every second, but no one seemed to care.

"Please! Please, I beg you! She needs me; she needs to see me when she wakes up. Don't do this to her. Don't hurt your daughter more than you already have!" Mei pleaded, and her voice fainted as her body was dragged to the castle's prison.

The hallway went silent again, but the faint cries of Mei remained within the walls of the castle.

Daiyu witnessed everything, but she chose to stay quiet. Maybe it was her sorrow and shock that took over her body and made her numb, or maybe the pinch of jealousy sealed her lips. She knew every word that Mei had said was true, but she also knew that the truth was more brutal to accept and easier to overlook.

The doctor finally came out and told them the surprisingly positive news. Xiuying was going to live! Daiyu was relieved, and she rushed inside the room, holding her daughter's hand.

"Oh, Xiuying! Mommy is here now!"

Xiuying slowly opened her eyes and looked around. "Where's Mei? Why are you here?" she asked.

"Mei is gone. I'm here now, your mother," Daiyu replied, and she held onto her hand tightly.

But Xiuying moved her hand away and guardedly said, "You are *not* my mother. You have never been, and you will never be."

The words that Daiyu heard from her daughter left her in a state of agony. She felt like someone took the meaning of her existence away, and she started to step back slowly in disbelief from what she had just heard.

You're not my mother. You're not my mother. Quiet

whispers were on repeat in her mind, and before she realized, Daiyu fainted and fell.

Qianfan witnessed the scene, and the moment he saw Daiyu fall onto the floor, he decided that it was time for Xiuying to leave, and this time, forever. Everyone rushed to Daiyu's aid. Qianfan carried her in his arms and took her into their bedroom.

Daiyu remained unconscious for hours, but when she woke up, she was petrified, shaking like a crumbling leaf.

"I-I, s-she said I am n-not her mother!" Daiyu cried, and Qianfan could only comfort her. "I never want to see her again, Qianfan. She doesn't need me," she stuttered, sobbing as she rested her shoulder on Qianfan's arm.

He held her tight because he knew that nothing he'd say could make her feel better, but she said what he wanted to hear, and now, he was going to make sure that Xiuying's existence vanished from their lives. Forever.

"That child will no longer hurt my wife," he said as he summoned the chief royal guard. "You must take Xiuying away, somewhere miles and a full sea away from this kingdom, and you must leave her there. Give her some supplies, but nothing more," Qianfan ordered.

"But what if she dies there?" the chief asked.

"Are you questioning my orders?"

"Apologies, and yes, my king," the chief guard replied.

"Take her away at dawn," Qianfan continued, and the guard obeyed.

A small island that had been abandoned for decades, off in the Pacific Ocean. That was where they'd send her. It was surrounded by nothing but water, and the atmosphere was damp. There was nothing on the island but dead trees and sand, with a few large boulders scattered here and there.

It would take three days by sea just to get there. So, the preparations for departure began, baskets of food were prepared, barrels of drinking water were loaded onto the ship, and a group of five maids, ten guards, and five soldiers were going to escort Xiuying, almost as if they were preparing for another funeral. Because their plan was to leave her there to die.

And all while everyone was getting ready, Xiuying was oblivious to what was happening. Her mind was clouded with questions. It had been two days, and Mei was nowhere to be seen. And no one was allowed to tell her what had happened, keeping her locked in her room as they prepared to ship her away.

"Open the door! Open the door!" she screamed and banged against it, but there was no one around to hear her plea. "Please, I need to see Mei. You can't keep me locked away forever!" she shouted again, and suddenly, the door creaked opened. It was Qianfan.

"Calm down, you stupid child," he said with a smirk. "Don't worry, you won't be staying here for long." He paused and entered the room, his eyes looking around the pale walls and her desk.

Xiuying was stunned; she couldn't move or utter a single word. This was the first time her father had said anything to her, and even if she hated him, her heart started to beat faster and faster when she saw him. The castle's maids all piled into Xiuying's room and started to pack up her things into wooden crates.

"What? What's happening?" Xiuying asked.

"You are going away. I cannot allow you to hurt my family anymore. Besides, you told Daiyu that she is no longer your mother, and because of that, you no longer have a place in this kingdom," Qianfan replied, the calmness in his voice sending shivers down Xiuying's spine.

"But, Father..." She couldn't even bring herself to complete her sentence, unsure of what to say.

"I am *not* your father. I never was, and I am *never* going to be," Qianfan replied as he stared into her eyes, eyes that were watery with tears.

Qianfan strolled over to the window, admiring the view while the maids packed her things, and Xiuying begged for them to stop.

"Please leave my things. Don't do this, please! Mei!" She sobbed and cried out, "Mei, where are you?!"

Qianfan turned toward her with a sneer. "Oh, haven't you heard? Mei is no longer here. You are *never* going to see her again. You made the mistake of hurting my wife, and you will pay for it for the rest of your life. Take her away!" And he waved them off.

Xiuying resisted and pushed the maids away, but no matter how hard she tried, she was much too weak.

And after a few minutes of struggling, she fell unconscious.

The weather was rowdy, the winds racing, the trees rushing back and forth, the birds struggling to find their way, and the dark clouds above getting ready to shower over the kingdom of secrets. This time, the dawn was bringing darkness, and nobody knew what was ahead.

Xiuying was carried by two maids while she was still unconscious and placed in a carriage that would take her to the shipping port. The carriage started to move, and the child woke up, but was too weak and emotionally exhausted to move or make a sound. Her eyes opened a bit, but all she could see was the castle shrinking in the background as the carriage moved forward.

And just as Xiuying saw the castle shrinking, Mei saw a carriage leaving the castle and traveling down a road toward the seaside from her small window in the prison cell, but she didn't know who it was.

It was all a blur to the small child. One second, her eyes would open slightly, and the next, they would turn dark. She could faintly see the blue of the sea, the dark-colored waves, a giant wooden boat, and tons of wooden crates. She felt numb and lost consciousness again as she was carried onto the ship.

At the same time, Daiyu wasn't doing much better. She woke up with contractions, cramps, and went into premature labor once again, but this time, she didn't have Mei by her side. And yet again, Qianfan was there with the hopes of having a baby boy, curiously waiting outside the room after shipping their first child to the depths of despair. History was repeating itself, and Daiyu feared what it would bring. She prayed that another girl would not come out for the sake of both her and the child's life. She knew Qianfan loved her, but he could *never* love a daughter.

Daiyu was struggling during the procedure. It almost felt like she didn't want to bring this child into existence. She was aching with sharp pains, and it intensified as the clock continued to tick.

The silence in the hallway broke as cries of a baby were heard after seven hours of immense labor pains, and as a result, Daiyu was left in comatose, not knowing the gender of her child. Qianfan bolted into the room, and to his surprise, it was... another girl. His second-born was *also* a daughter, and he knew he couldn't get away with pronouncing her dead, not again. All eyes were on this royal birth, and the kingdom was eager to welcome a new child.

Qianfan slowly walked out of the room. He couldn't even look at his daughter or Daiyu. He made his way toward the main terrace and stood there as the thunder roared above him, and sprinkles of rain started to fall.

"How is this possible?" he asked himself in disbelief. "What have I done to deserve this? Is this karma? I send Xiuying away, and now she is reborn? What can I do to get a son? I deserve a son! Xiuying has brought nothing but terrible luck to my honor. She has ruined my life!" He shouted, looking toward the ocean, "It's all because of you!" And he grabbed the vase beside him and slammed it against the wall.

CHAPTER FOUR

XIUYING WOKE UP TO FIND HERSELF LYING IN A SMALL RUSTY room. It had an uneven wooden floor, a single mattress with off-white sheets, a warm blanket, and two small round windows on the wall in front of her that only had a view of the aggressive ocean waves. The light in the room was a dull sunset orange, and it smelled like burning candles and drenched wood.

The floor creaked as she stood up and walked toward one of the windows. Everything seemed so uncertain, and she had no idea what was ahead, what was going to happen to her. She had cried, screamed, and yelled so much that now, she couldn't feel anything. All she had left were untangled thoughts, and she questioned herself.

"How am I always the problem, no matter where I go? I tried to end my life, and that too, became a problem. Is my gender my only flaw? Such an injustice to my parents? Maybe if I had welcomed my mother with open arms while she was beside me, I wouldn't be here right now; maybe she would've taken me under her wing instead. And Mei, she just disappeared on me. I trusted her, and she just left me. I don't even know who to trust anymore."

Her thoughts were interrupted as she fell onto the wooden floor. The ship was struggling to fight the strong waves caused by the storm. Things around her started to slide from one end of the room to the other, and the candle lights were flickering. Her heart sank and feared that the ship would, too.

DAIYU REGAINED CONSCIOUSNESS TO RECEIVE THE disheartening news that she had given birth to another daughter.

"This world is a treacherous and lonely place, especially if you're born a daughter in this castle," she whispered to her baby. "I'm afraid I cannot fight for you. Qianfan is too powerful; he will never allow it." She had given up hope that Qianfan would accept the little girl as his after what he'd done to Xiuying, and she prepared herself for what's to come next.

It was dusk, and Qianfan finally decided to see Daiyu. He entered their room. His gaze wandered around until he saw Daiyu resting on their bed with silks sheets, pillows around her, and their daughter in her arms. Qianfan walked closer and sat on the bed's corner.

"So? What have you decided?" Daiyu asked in a low voice.

"Nothing; my thoughts are conflicted. She's not what I wanted or expected. Disappointment is all I can feel right now," Qianfan stated with his eyes glued to the floor and with a voice that had lost its firmness.

"Perhaps, in disappointment, we are perfectly matched. I was a fool to think that you'd welcome our child with open arms," Daiyu replied.

"You know, I never want to hurt you or break your heart, Daiyu."

"Tell me, my dear, does a heart still break if it has stopped beating?" Daiyu asked while looking down at her newborn.

Qianfan stayed quiet. Although it felt like history was repeating itself, and Daiyu was prepared for another compromise, Qianfan felt different. He felt conflicted, and under the impression that he was only cursed with a daughter because he'd mistreated Xiuying. He'd sent her away, and Daiyu wasn't even aware of it yet.

The silence in their room grew as the hours ticked

into the night, and Qianfan's thoughts grew louder. He assumed karma was coming back for revenge, and in order to receive a son next time, he'd have to change his ways.

"Maybe if I treat my daughter right this time, I'll be gifted with the blessing of a son," he told himself and tried to fall asleep.

BUT FOR XIUYING, THE NIGHT GOT PERTURBED. SHE DIDN'T know if the ship would make it to their destination without meeting an unfortunate event. The sky lit with thunder, the windows flashing, and all she could hear were waves crashing into each other. She was horrified, scared out of her wits, and even though she had wanted to die, the thought of dying alone, afraid, with no one to find her, terrified her.

It was also in this moment that she realized that, although she was being sent away and abandoned, this change was the next chapter in her life. It was going to be a new and different experience for her. It was time for her to move on and leave what had already left her. This was still a chance for her to start over, to build for herself the life that she'd always wanted. And lucky enough, the storm soon passed, the clouds bidding farewell, and her heart settled.

"Tomorrow's going to be a fresh start for me; it's time to leave everything behind," she told herself, wrapped herself in the blanket, and closed her eyes to fall asleep.

The next morning, the sky had turned a bright blue. Xiuying opened her eyes to see rays of sunshine entering her room through the round windows. The aura in her room felt different. It felt happier, as if the storm really *did* brush all the sorrow away.

She rolled out of bed and got dressed. She'd been locked away in this room for the past two days, and something in her made her feel like she was going to get out of here today. Over the past two days, she barely ate a thing, even though all the dishes that the maid dropped off for her were her favorites.

Today, the breakfast that she received was congee with green onions. This reminded her of Mei, but she tried to push away her thoughts, tried not to think of her. She still couldn't understand why Mei had disappeared, but she suspected that it had something to do with her father.

"I hope you are well, wherever you are. Even if there *is* a possibility that you left on your own. I will cherish your memory forever as the guardian who looked over me," she addressed Mei and said out loud.

As she dug into the bowl of congee, the warmth bringing life back into her, someone knocked on her door and slid a folded piece of paper toward her. She was surprised to see it there and couldn't understand who on this ship would write her a note. She leaned down and picked up the sheet.

THE NEW DAWN BROUGHT A BRIGHT LIGHT INTO THE CASTLE, too. The angry storm had left, flowers were in full blossom, and the grass looked greener. Daiyu opened her eyes and couldn't believe what she was seeing. Qianfan was holding their newborn daughter in his arms and smiled as he swaddled her. Daiyu rushed out of bed and stood there in shock.

"Qianfan?" she called over to him.

"Good morning, my sunshine. You are finally up! She was crying, so I picked her up. She looks just like you."

Daiyu was confused. She didn't know if she should be happy that he finally understood, or sad that his arrogance and dignity cost her their first child.

"So, what does this mean, Qianfan?" Daiyu found herself asking.

Qianfan walked toward her and handed their daughter to Daiyu. "I couldn't sleep last night because of something I did, and it made me realize that karma is haunting us. We need to fix things and do things the right way with our second daughter, so that we get a son next time. I promise you that we're going to give her everything she needs, love, admiration, time, us. She is going to be celebrated, and I promise that we will keep her close." Qianfan smiled.

Daiyu was still stunned, but disappointed at the same time because Qianfan thought a daughter meant bad karma. But still, he was willing to do everything for her and their new child, so she kept her worries to herself.

"That's great, Qianfan, and that makes me really happy. Finally, I get to be a mother, and we get to be a family," she said, and Qianfan nodded. "So, what made you realize this?"

"It's because I sent Xiuying away, far away from the castle. She hurt you, and us, and we needed her gone. But don't worry. She's safe. We'll just never see her again."

Daiyu fell silent. She wanted to scream, to blame her husband for all the pain in Xiuying's life, for sending away her child, but she couldn't. She'd become numb to anything related to her first daughter. Besides, she had another child now, and it was time to move on.

The next day, Qianfan and Daiyu got dressed in their finest garments and announced the birth of their daughter. They didn't give her the title of *princess*, but they called for a celebration and welcomed her in front of the entire kingdom. Visitors started to pour in, and the castle was filled with flowers, bouquets, and presents for the newborn.

Daiyu was over the moon. She felt important, she felt loved, and she felt like a mother. Qianfan has announced a grand ball, a celebration for their daughter, and had invited everyone to come. The castle was decorated with fresh white lilies and baby pink roses. There were ten main courses prepared and six different types of dessert on the menu, and it felt like serenity was in the air, and happiness had taken over the castle.

But there was one person who could not understand the sudden change in Qianfan's mindset. Qiang was suspicious of him and eager to get to the root of the reason that led Qianfan to open his heart to his second daughter.

THE PARTY WAS IN FULL SWING AT THE CASTLE, BUT MILES away, trapped in a ship, curiosity had taken over Xiuying. She sat down on her bed, unfolded the note, and started to read.

To the little girl who is entering a new chapter in her life,

This new journey that you are entering is going to test you in every way possible. It is going to test your hope, patience, strength, and beliefs. You have always been a little girl who tries to overcome every obstacle that life puts in your way. In the end, you always win. You are always able to pick yourself up, and that's the most special thing about you. You are moving to a new place. Make this place your home. If you welcome it with an open heart, I promise you, it will give you the love, admiration, respect, and the sense of belongingness that you have always wanted.

I know that life has been tough for you, but do not let that change you as a person. Always be the person who cares, the one who makes the effort, loves without any hesi-

tation. Be the person who bears it all for those who cannot. Be the one who never shies away from her feelings. Be the one who sees the good in everyone. If you do, you will only receive goodness in return. There is nothing stronger than a person who stays soft to a world that has never been kind to them.

You kept going, even when the world was against you, even when no one was on your side. You never gave up hope. I hope you never stop doing that, and I hope you know that I am proud of you.

Writing about your feelings always helps, so don't stop writing, especially when you are not able to understand how you feel. Even if you don't get a reply to your written notes, write them for yourself, and don't keep your feelings locked in your heart.

Your new life awaits you!

Farewell,

Your Well-Wisher

Tears welled up in her eyes, but this time, they were tears of happiness. She felt like someone was looking after her, and it made her feel less alone. She received the note from inside the ship, which meant that whoever her Well-Wisher was, was on board, and she was eager to see their face. She wanted to cherish this letter forever, so she folded it into a small square and kept it safe in a box that she knew she would take with her. Suddenly, the door of her room started to unlock, and someone opened it.

The kingdom was excitedly waiting to see the newborn's face. The ball had started, and after a few minutes, Qianfan appeared with Daiyu and their newborn child in her arms. They were showered with flowers as they walked toward their throne. When they sat down, a guard came in with the magic stone. The child was going to be marked with the stone to give her the magical power, just like they had done with Xiuying.

As the guard approached the throne, Qianfan held the magic stone in front of everyone and began to say those same words. "From blood to blood and the bond it creates, mark what differentiates us from the rest of the mates." As he recited, the stone glowed when he placed it on his daughter's arm and left a mark.

Everyone cheered and applauded while the room lit up with the stone's glow, and Qianfan spoke, "Here, in front of the entire kingdom, we name our daughter, Xiaofan."

As the kingdom celebrated the birth of a sibling that Xiuying would never come to know, the door opened, and Xiuying saw a lanky, tall man, who appeared in his sixties, standing in front of her. He had a fair complexion, brown eyes, and black hair. He was dressed in a military uniform that was worn by the majors in the army.

"Can I speak to you for a second, Xiuying?" he asked.

"Who are you?" Xiuying asked.

The man came inside and answered, "I am the major your father appointed to escort you to the island. My name is Huizhong, and you might know me as your Well-Wisher."

Xiuying's mouth dropped open, and her eyes glowed with joy as soon as she heard him.

"Xiuying, I am sorry for what you have been through, and I regret that I had to be the one to take you away from the castle."

"It's okay, Huizhong. It wasn't your fault," Xiuying replied, paused, and then asked, "I wrote to you back at the castle. Why didn't you respond?"

"Your father was growing suspicious as to what I was doing, and I had to stop. If he knew that I was in contact with you, he would have done worse to me than what he had done to Mei. I empathize with you, my child, but I could not put you or myself at risk."

He sighed and moved toward the window.

"Mei? What happened to her?" Xiuying stammered while she stood behind Huizhong.

"You don't know? She fought for you. She went against all odds and said what needed to be said to the king and queen, but that only landed her in jeopardy," he mumbled as he turned to face Xiuying.

"Jeopardy?" Xiuying questioned.

"There is a lot that you do not know, Little One. But Mei loves you, and she did everything she could for you. Qianfan has sentenced her to life in prison because she talked back and questioned the intentions of the royal family. There's nothing anyone could do to help her."

Xiuying regretted having ever doubted the intentions of Mei. She felt overwhelmed with guilt and sorrow, for blaming her for getting her shipped away. It wasn't Mei's fault at all.

"This would never have happened if I hadn't attempted to end my life," she lamented.

"Oh, no, Little One, it is *not* your fault. It was all written and meant to be; it would have happened with or without what you did. Do not take yourself as a prisoner for the unfortunate event. Mei will always love you; she always has. All she wants for you is happiness. I visited her in the prison before we left, and the first question she asked was about you, how you were doing. She would want you to have a regret-free life."

Xiuying could no longer control her emotions, and she started to cry.

"My dear, you have to live your life for her. Wipe your tears away, Little One. Keep your head up, and I promise you that what's ahead is better than what you've left," he continued.

She wiped her tears and asked, "Where are you taking me?"

"I am taking you to where your father ordered me

to take you. You are being sent to an island, completely stranded and surrounded by the ocean. Your father wanted you gone. He wanted you to suffer and make survival a challenge for you, hence, choosing an abandoned island. But what he doesn't know is that this place has some wonderful secrets and presence of people who are going to make your life flourish. Good things are ahead of you," he concluded with a smile on his face.

Xiuying was furious about everything her father had done, but she was looking forward to her new home and the countless possibilities it would bring.

"I have told you all of this because I want you to know that taking your past with you will only affect your future. You have to accept the truth and move on, my child," Huizhong continued as he sat beside her. "And I am *always* going to be here for you. I will come visit you whenever I have to travel. I will *always* be your Well-Wisher, Little One." And he hugged her.

Xiuying looked up at him and smiled. "I'm glad," she whispered.

"We will be arriving at the island today," he told her and left the room, leaving the door open.

Xiuying had a lot of things to understand and overcome, but she was grateful that even though the universe never treated her right, it kept on sending people who looked over her.

"This is a sign to move on and start a new life," she told herself as she began to pack up her things.

It seemed like times were changing, and for the better. Daiyu looked out the window and let the warmth of the sun touch her face as she held Xiaofan in her arms. The happiness that Xiaofan brought her made her forget all about Xiuying, not thinking about her even once ever since Qianfan accepted Xiaofan. Qianfan then came into the room with flowers and Daiyu's favorite dessert.

"I come bearing presents, my queen!" He laughed.

Daiyu turned around and saw Qianfan in a rather pleasant mood.

"Thank you, my king!" she exclaimed, her cheeks turning rosy.

Qianfan leaned forward and held Xiaofan in his arms. "Seems like everyone loves her already. The kingdom is celebrating her birth more than we are. I am already getting marriage proposals for her for when she grows up." He sighed with delight, and after a few seconds, his voice suddenly changed as he said, "Things would have been different, happier, if she were a boy."

Daiyu smiled and ignored his words, concentrating on the dessert that she was stuffing into her mouth and not the sentence that Qianfan had just uttered.

There were two knocks on the door before Qiang walked in. She'd been confused ever since Qianfan accepted his second daughter. She didn't understand why her son had changed his mind about wanting a son, and she needed to understand what he was thinking. So, she requested to meet with him in person... without Daiyu.

Qianfan kissed his wife and child on the forehead before walking out into the garden with his mother. The sun was about the set, allowing the dusk to take over the sky.

"Are you happy? How did your demeanor just change overnight? You abandoned your firstborn and sent her miles away, and now you welcome the second daughter with open arms?" Qiang interrogated.

"Oh, Mother, I do not expect you to understand, but Daiyu is happy, and her happiness matters to me," he replied.

"How come her happiness didn't matter to you before? When she begged you to accept your own child? Enough with the act! You might be able to fool everyone else, but it's *not* going to work on your own mother!" she declared.

Qianfan wasn't fond of his mother asking him questions. He hated it when Qiang tried to parent him.

He sighed. "Mother, I need a son, and in order to do that, I have to treat this daughter of mine right, whether I like it or not. I have to. Or else karma is going to keep providing me with daughters. I am not fooling anyone. I'm just trying to keep Daiyu happy so I don't lose my mind. I don't expect you to understand." Then he continued, "And I certainly don't want you to treat my daughter in any way that hurts her. Do not resent her, and I mean it!" he declared and walked off without listening to what Qiang had to say.

Qiang was left in a state of disbelief. Qianfan was standing up for his daughter, even if it was for all the wrong reasons. She also didn't appreciate the tone that he'd used with her, especially in front of all the guards.

"How dare he disrespect me like that?" she snapped and promised herself to teach him a lesson when she got the chance.

Although the door to Xiuying's room was unlocked, she couldn't bring herself to go out and explore the ship that she had been on for the past three days. The tiny room she had been confined in became her comfort zone. She had experienced her darkest days inside it, yet also her brightest. The place that gave her goosebumps now brought her comfort, and she couldn't stop thinking about Mei. She wanted to make things right with her, but she knew that could never happen.

The level of hatred she had for her parents had reached an extreme. Her eyes twitched around her room, and she saw her writing quill that she kept on top of a box.

"Maybe I can write one last note to her. Mei always

told me to say or write what I felt, and maybe she needs this more than I do."

She got up from her bed and opened the lid of the wooden box, took out her scrolls and ink, then grabbed the quill and sat down at the rusty table beside her and began to write.

My beloved Mei,

Your prayers and blessings have saved me once again. I am well and in good hands. You do not have to worry about my well-being anymore, Mei. You have worried and compromised enough. I know what you did for me, and I cannot believe that someone would give their life up for me, but maybe that's what mothers do. You are my mother, and no one can change that, even if we are miles apart.

You have helped me become the best version of myself. You have helped me turn my weaknesses into strengths. And you have taught me to believe in myself. You told me that you were always going to be there for me, and you have proven that. Thank you for everything that you have done for me, for every compromise that you have made, and for putting me before everyone else, even yourself.

I wish I could've seen you before I was sent away, but maybe saying goodbye would have been much harder. So, this is for the best, I guess. I finally found out who my Well-Wisher is. He is here with me, and his presence, his words, remind me of you. He's like a male version of you, Mei. You'll know who it is when you get this letter. He's looking out for me and has promised me that the place I am going to will become my new home. I am not scared. I am looking forward to this new chapter in my life. Leaving the castle and you was not my choice, but whatever happens from this point on, is. I will make sure to make every second of my life worth living for, for you and for myself.

I will keep writing to you, Mei. I know that you won't get my letters after this one, but writing to you will always make me feel like I am connected to you. So, I promise that whenever happiness or sorrow reaches my soul, I will always write them down. I will always tell you, even if I don't get a response. I will always keep our memories in my heart, Mother, and I hope you do, too. I'll always remember you. Hopefully, one day, we can meet again. I promise I will never forget you until then.

Love you forever,

Xiuying

She experienced a sudden wave of relief after writing down what she'd felt, almost like she was bidding Mei a farewell, and this was the end of something beautiful. Xiuying folded the note, placed it inside the scroll, and sealed it by dripping candle wax onto the lid. She decided to then go and find Huizhong.

She opened the door and heard a faint creak. She then found a winding stairway that led toward the deck, and she started to walk until she found herself standing on the deck of the ship, the small island only a short distance away. Her eyes wandered around, and she found Huizhong standing to her right, admiring the sun. She could feel the other maids and guards staring at her as she made her way over to him.

"Hi," she gasped softly.

"Hey, you made it outside. Delighted to see you, Little One!" he replied. "Look at the sunset, the sun leaving without any hesitation, welcoming the dark because it knows that time will bring it back... and that's exactly what our lives are like, a pattern of light and dark. We have to let them take over us sometimes because we have to experience different emotions. How else will we experience joy unless we know what sorrow feels like?"

Xiuying smiled and replied, "That's very insightful. I have never looked at it like that."

She moved her hand forward and handed over the scroll.

"What's this?" he asked with great curiosity.

"I wrote something for Mei. Can you please help me give it to her?" she asked.

"Of course, I will hand this over to her myself, and I'm sure she'll be delighted to hear from you."

Xiuying stayed quiet and let the moment sink in. She gazed at the changing colors of the sky as the cold breeze slowly touched her hair, chasing the ship's rumble.

"I want to remember this moment forever," she whispered to herself.

"Xiuying, I know that you've been through a lot, and at a very young age at that, but don't let that define you. Don't let the bad experiences speak for who you are. You are more than that, kind, affectionate, and talented. Let the good things take over, and let people see you for who you actually are, not for the bad things that have happened to you."

Xiuying agreed. She knew that people only sympathized with her, felt sorry for her, and she never liked that. She had a chance now to change how people saw her, and she decided never to bring up anything from her past to anyone she'd meet.

"Yes, you're right. Happy people are the best kind of people, aren't they?" she asked.

"Hm, maybe not the *best* kind, but they *are* more preferable," Huizhong said, and they both chuckled. "We're about to reach the island. You should go and pack up your things."

When Xiuying got back to her room, she sat down on her bed. Her life was about to change, and hopefully, for the better. Although she was optimistic, excited, and looked forward to what was ahead, she was also scared. She was going to be on her own for the first time in her life. Mei wasn't going to be there, and her Well-Wisher would not be by her side. She knew she had to be brave, but how?

On the bright side, Qianfan and Daiyu weren't going to be there either, and that was a blessing in and of itself. As much as she tried to put herself in a healthy mindset, deep down, she knew that the memories of her past would come back from time to time, and they would affect her.

The ship spontaneously stopped and caused her to stumble onto her butt. She got up, dusted off the clothes that she was wearing, stood up, and realized that they had reached the island. She was wearing a dark pink dress with off-white embroidered sleeves and flowery cufflinks, and she tied her hair back with a white ribbon. She looked like royalty, the royalty that she now hated.

Huizhong knocked on the door, letting her know that it was time to leave. She opened the door and welcomed him in.

"Saying goodbye to the room?" he asked.

She laughed. "Yeah, I think I'll actually miss this place."

Huizhong looked at her. "Well, that's surprising."

"This journey has been insightful for me. There's a lot I have learned and overcome. As much as I want to hate the experience, I will *always* be grateful for it."

Huizhong stepped closer to her and sighed. "There is something that you need to know before you leave."

"And... that is?"

"Every child in your family is given a magical power, and that includes you. You were marked with the stone when you were born, and now you are old enough to understand how to use it," he said, and Xiuying listened. "Here, give me your hand."

Xiuying hesitated, but she reached over.

"Look at this mark on your wrist. It's a tiny flower engraved onto your skin. I cannot say for sure what your power is, but it has something to do with the Earth and its four elements. Earth, water, air, and fire. This power has been given to you. It exists inside of you. You just have to recognize it, feel the connection with it, and accept the power that the stone has bestowed upon you."

Xiuying looked down at her wrist and stood there, shocked. "I always thought this was a birthmark, and it meant nothing."

"It means everything, Xiuying. Generations upon generations of your family have been gifted with magical powers. Your father has control over the sun and moon, and your mother can communicate with animals. Your ancestors have made legacies for controlling the elements. Every newborn brings a new and different gift." Huizhong recalled and continued, "And it is rumored that the firstborn gets the most powerful gift. You are the firstborn, and you are *always* going to be more powerful than any of your siblings, no matter who or what they are."

Xiuying stayed silent for a moment before saying, "Maybe that's why father wanted his firstborn to be a boy."

"Maybe," Huizhong replied. "Remember to believe in yourself and your power," he added, and then it was time to leave. "Let's go, Xiuying. It's time."

He smiled at her and left the room.

Xiuying took a deep breath and looked around the tiny room, the round windows, the small rusty bed, and the tiny table on which she wrote the farewell note for Mei. This was a life-changing event for her. And now it was time to leave everything behind and start over.

The maids started to come into her room to

transfer the wooden crates to the deck. After all the crates had been moved, Xiuying gave the room one last look and slowly closed the door. She walked upstairs and saw all the hustle. The deck was crowded with maids and guards, moving things back and forth, and the sun had almost disappeared.

The island looked beautiful but rugged. There were mountains surrounding. They were so tall that they made her feel even smaller than she already was. But there wasn't anything green on the island, nothing but sand and dead branches.

"How can I survive here?" she asked herself, but then realized that she had no other choice.

Huizhong tapped on her shoulder and asked her if he could escort her off the ship and onto the island. Xiuying agreed, and they both got off the ship. He strictly told all the other guards and maids to stay on the ship. No one was permitted to step another foot onto the island.

It was getting dark, and Xiuying felt scared.

"Are you going to leave me here alone? There's no one else here. I-I'll die out here!" she stuttered.

"Have patience, Xiuying. This place is not what it seems; there is more than what meets the eye. Follow me," he replied.

She followed him quietly with worries that she could not dispel. She could see the mountains all around them. There were dead plants and shabby bushes, the land was infertile, and she could feel, with every step, dry branches being crushed beneath her feet. The ambience, the cold breeze, the night taking over, brought shivers down her spine; she grew pale, and her heart was racing.

She followed Huizhong, and suddenly, he stopped in front of a cave that had a dim light at the end of it.

"Remember what we talked about, okay?" he asked and entered the cave.

Xiuying hesitated at first, but she had no other choice but to follow him. The cave was dark, and she noticed tiny red eyes when she looked above her, before realizing that they were bats. She hissed but stayed quiet.

"Am I going to live in a cave for the rest of my life? So much for a new life," she said to herself sarcastically.

CHAPTER FIVE

After walking for several minutes, they reached the other side of the cave. Xiuying was looking down at her feet to avoid staring at the bats, and as soon as she looked up again, her eyes lit up.

She smiled with a sigh of relief; there was an entire civilization right in front of her, a small cottage town hidden and protected by the mountains.

The mountains were only surrounding the village, and they acted almost as a decoy. The streets were lit up by fire lanterns. They were bright, warm, and most importantly, welcoming. There were small cottages around every corner, with a small porch, oversized windows, wooden doors, and they were painted a dusty brown pastel color.

The streets felt alive with small children running around, and there were colorful decorations everywhere. Dark blue flags with flowers on them hung at every corner, the sky was a shade of dark blue and purple, and the view of the village was heartwarming. It was a small town where everyone knew each other and showed up for one another during times of need.

"Welcome to Naje." Huizhong smiled and squeezed Xiuying's hand. "I told you this place was more than what meets the eye, Little One." He chuckled with joy.

"Ha, you were right." Xiuying giggled beside him as they walked down the cobblestone pathway.

She couldn't get enough of the village. It left her in awe, the children playing marbles, the smell of freshly-baked bread, the aroma of love in the air; she loved every bit of it.

"Huizhong!" an elderly voice called out with admiration. "You are finally here; we have been waiting for you."

Xiuying turned around and saw a woman nearing her late eighties. She had braided white hair and tiny yellow flowers in them. She had wrinkles on her face, a fair complexion, and a lovely smile. She reached out and gave Huizhong a hug.

"It's so good to see you, Huizhong. You look well, my son!" she gushed.

"Oh, Hua, it's so good to see you as well. This is Xiuying, the girl I told you about."

"Yes, yes. Xiuying, my dear, you are so beautiful, and we are glad that you are here. It's about time I have some company. With Huizhong gone, it gets pretty lonely." She laughed while hugging Xiuying tightly.

Xiuying beamed and said, "Thank you for having me."

"Oh, no need to be polite, my dear. You are too kind," Hua replied with an upbeat tone and added, "Let's get you settled in. Come on. Let me show you your new home."

Xiuying and Huizhong followed her as she made her way through the lively streets of the village. After a short walk, they reached her cottage. It was the same as all the other ones, with a large wooden door, a front porch, and gigantic windows.

But there was one thing that stood out about her cottage. There was a tree with tiny yellow flowers all over it. It was the only one like it, from what Xiuying had seen in the village. Hua opened the cottage door and led them inside. It was beautiful on the inside. The place had an aroma of cherry blossom trees and fresh cookies, floral murals hung on the walls, and wooden furniture covered with soft, colorful cushions sat around the open rooms. There were three bedrooms in the cottage, a living room, and an open kitchen.

Of the three rooms, one belonged to Hua, and one was a library. The third room was given to Xiuying, already decorated with peach-colored paintings of flowers all over the center wall, and the lightest shade of pastel pink paint was used on the other three walls. Her room had a large window with off-white curtains on it, and she could see the street and other homes at the base of the mountains. There was also a desk in her room with some books on it and a light lantern, along with a small bed that was covered with a quilt and had a fluffy pillow on it.

"Do you like it?" Hua asked in hesitation.

"Like? I love it! Thank you, Hua." Xiuying sighed with joyful tears in her eyes.

"Alright, my dear. I'm glad you do. The villagers will bring your things here first thing in the morning, okay?" Hua said.

"Okay." Xiuying blushed.

"Now, let me make you both something to eat!" Hua turned to Huizhong and raised a brow at him. But he shook his head.

"No, I can't. I have to leave. I only came here to escort Xiuying, and now it's time for me to go."

Xiuying looked at Huizhong like she didn't want him to leave, but she knew she had to say goodbye to him. He, too, had to leave, as everyone else did. Huizhong thanked Hua as she showered him with her blessings and said her farewell.

Xiuying took a deep breath and walked toward Huizhong.

"Can we talk outside for a bit?" she asked him, and he nodded his head in agreement. "Thank you for doing this, for bringing me here and not leaving me stranded as my father told you to," Xiuying murmured when they got outside.

Huizhong laughed and asked, "Did you really think I was going to leave you stranded? I came here with a plan, Little One. I have known Hua for ages, and I promise you, you are in good hands. I am your Well-Wisher, after all. I have to live up to the title, right?"

Xiuying sniffed and replied, "Ha, right. So, how do you know Hua?"

"Six years ago, I was on a voyage and encountered a problem with my ship. I had to anchor it here, on this very island. While the rest of my crew stayed on to try and repair it, I got out to explore the island. That's how I found Hua, injured. Sharp rocks had wounded her foot, and blood flowed from her wound. I tried to help her as best as I could. I wrapped up the wound with my shirt and helped her to her cottage. After that, she always welcomed me with open arms, and I've always seen her as a motherly figure. But she made me promise to never mention the village to anyone else. No one else knows that they live here. They chose to disconnect from the rest of the world, happy with their own kind without any invaders. I try to visit Hua every now and then, once every six months or so."

"And what about her family? Does she have children?" Xiuying asked.

"Her husband died five years ago. He was a

wonderful man who kept her happy. And after his death, her only son left the village because he wanted to explore life beyond these mountains. He left without realizing the worth of this place or his own mother, and Hua has been alone ever since." Then he added, "I wrote a letter to her, telling her about you, before we started our journey. She's excited to have you live here with her. She needs you as much as you need her."

"I already love her." Xiuying smiled. "And I love this village."

"I'm not sure when I will come back, Xiuying. But I will come back one day; this is my promise to you. Focus on yourself from now on. You have everything you need, and you will get everything you want here. It's time for me to leave now before the crew gets suspicious; everyone thinks I am leaving you in the wilderness," he told Xiuying.

She nodded. "I'll miss you. Take care of yourself, and don't forget to give my scroll to Mei, please."

"I will miss you, too, Little One. Stay happy, and I won't forget. I will deliver it to Mei myself." He hugged her.

"Alright, goodbye. Have a safe journey," she said, and Huizhong smiled before he left.

Xiuying watched as he walked away, a tear or two trickling down her cheek. He turned halfway back, saw her standing, and waved goodbye. But then he disappeared, and just like that, Xiuying's Well-Wisher was gone, and her new life was about to start. She walked back to her cottage and opened the door. During the time when she was gone, Hua had prepared all sorts of goodies for her, from cookies to baked bread to her favorite red bean cake.

"Oh! You're home," Hua exclaimed with excitement when Xiuying entered.

"Yes, I am home." She humbly smiled.

XIUYING WOKE UP THE NEXT MORNING, SLOWLY OPENED HER eyes, and caught a glimpse of the warm sunlight coming through her bedroom window. She smiled, thinking to herself that her life would only change for the better from now on. She sat up and moved her eyes around her room. The painted flowers on the walls, the aroma of freshly-baked waffles—all made her fall in love with the place once again.

"Oh, my child. You're up! Just in time for breakfast. I made you waffles with chocolate syrup. Come on, rise and shine!" Hua sang.

"Thanks, Hua. I'll be right there," Xiuying replied with a humble smile on her face.

She got out of bed and tidied her room. She liked everything neat and organized, always. She found her way to the dining table, and it had the most delicious-looking waffles placed on it, decorated with a vase at the center that featured yellow flowers.

Xiuying took her seat, and it felt like she had been

born all over again, but this time, the experience was going to be a pleasant one.

"I will take you to meet everyone today. You are staying here, so it'll be good for you to meet the rest of the villagers and make some friends, my dear," Hua said as she pulled up a chair and sat beside Xiuying.

"Yes, of course," she replied. "Although, I've never made friends my age. I'm not sure if I'll be able to or if they'll like me."

Hua grinned. "This is something you should not worry about. Just be yourself, and everyone is going to adore you. I promise."

"I hope so. Hua, I've noticed that there isn't much greenery around here. There's only one tree outside your home. Why is that?"

Hua took a deep breath and explained, "This island has had its own history, and not a pleasant one. A long time ago, a noble warrior was left on this island to die, the scorching heat and lack of fresh water and food making it nearly impossible for him to survive for long. He was being punished for something he didn't do, framed by his very own confidant to a royal king. His family eventually came looking for him, but found nothing but rotting bones that had dissolved into the sand. Most others would've left, but this family didn't. They didn't want to leave their son behind, and that's how our tiny village came to be. The family settled here in secrecy, and their loved ones, along with the community who believed in the soldier, joined them. However, the island is mostly barren. The mountains and sand make it very hard for us to harvest food. It's almost as if the island is still mourning the warrior's death, even after centuries. The tree outside my home is known as the Golden Tree of Hope. It is the only one here because it's the only one that'll remain alive. I take care of it, and it takes care of us by giving us hope. Maybe one day, our village will become Lǜhuà."

"Lǜhuà?" Xiuying repeated.

"Yes, it means *greenery*."

Xiuying was moved by the story she had just heard, and it brought goosebumps to her body. Her heart was beating fast, and she felt a tingling sensation in her fingers. The village with such pure souls living in it had such a dark past.

"Hua, do you believe the island will get its greenery back one day?" Xiuying asked.

"Yes, I put my trust in Mother Nature, my dear. Something, or someone, is going to help our island one day," Hua replied as she placed a tiny yellow flower from her tree in Xiuying's hair.

"This says you belong here, Xiuying. This yellow flower welcomes you into our family and our home. I just want you to know that I'm happy to have you here."

Xiuying hugged her with teary eyes, and Hua hugged back. Xiuying really *did* feel like she was home, finally. Hua reminded her of Mei, the same motherly warmth, and she realized how, even when things go wrong, she'll always have someone who will look after her without any hidden motives.

"Okay, then, get dressed. You have many people to meet, and I'm sure you'll love Meili!" Hua exclaimed.

Hua was the kind of person whom everyone knew and adored in the village, Xiuying quickly found out; she was known for her excellent baking skills, kindness, and helpful advice. Everyone in the village felt at home around her. It was who she was, and she loved it. She knew the impact she had on people, and she used it to her advantage. She had many connections, and people would listen to her like she was some sort of prophet.

And now that Xiuying was with Hua, she too, had a special place in everyone's eyes. She barely knew anyone, but everyone already knew her. Hua packed some baked cookies for her closest friend's family and left the house to meet them. Xiuying, of course, followed her. She wore a light pink, knee-length dress with puffy sleeves that had tiny white flowers printed all over the fabric. This particular dress always made her feel comfortable, confident, and it made her feel like the best version of herself, which she needed to be today. She wore matching pastel sandals, let her hair down, and placed the tiny yellow flower on the side of her head.

She stepped out and whispered, "Here we go," took a deep breath, and started to walk alongside Hua.

The sky was light blue with hints of white clouds that had faded. The sun was shining bright, but still warm, in a comforting way. As they walked down the street, Xiuying noticed that everyone stopped to greet

Hua. Hua introduced Xiuying as her adopted daughter to the other villagers, and they welcomed her with open arms. Xiuying was overwhelmed by the amount of love that she was already getting. They had only gone down two streets, and she had already gotten invites for both a tea party and brunch.

Hua and Xiuying finally reached Lifen's home. Lifen was Hua's childhood friend, and their families had moved to the island together several years back. Their friendship was solid; nothing could tear them apart. They laughed and cried together, and they shared with each other all their secrets. Hua even watched Lifen's daughter and granddaughter grow old right alongside her friend. They weren't just friends. They were like family to each other.

"Hua! You're here," Lifen screamed with delight and leaned in for a hug.

"And you brought your famous cookies!" her daughter, Yilin, added as Hua extended the basket to them.

"And you must be Xiuying. You might not be aware, but you are the talk of the town these days." Yilin chuckled as she welcomed Xiuying inside.

"I'm not a fan of attention, to be honest," Xiuying replied.

The interior of Lifen's home was the same as Hua's, almost identical. The walls had flowers painted on them, the furniture was wooden, and the color combination involved dark hues of white and blue. Yilin went into the kitchen to brew some tea, and Lifen accompanied Hua and Xiuying into the living room, as they sat by the window with a clear view of the mountains and the scattered blue sky.

"So, Xiuying, how do you like our little village so far? And how is our Hua treating you?" Lifen asked.

"Oh, Lifen. It's amazing. I was so lucky to end up here with Hua. She has been like a mother to me already. I am grateful for everything she's doing for me," Xiuying replied with a smile.

"There's no need to be such a kindred spirit, my dear. It's our duty now to look after you. Remember, we want you here. You're one of us now, and if anything ever happens to you, come straight to me, okay?" Hua reminded the child.

"Meili is going to adore you! I have a feeling you two are going to become the best of friends," Lifen chimed in.

The thought of having a best friend her age excited Xiuying. She never had one before, and often wondered what it felt like to have a friend whom she could share moments of happiness and despair with.

"Where is Meili, anyway?" Hua asked.

"She's at school, learning to read and write. She's going to be back any minute now," Yilin replied as she placed the tiny teacups on the center table, served with the cookies that Hua brought.

"Why don't you get Xiuying enrolled?" Lifen suggested.

"What do you think, Xiuying?" Hua looked at her and asked.

"I would love to."

Although Xiuying could already read and write as any normal adult could, she still said yes because she didn't want to give up on the chance to experience what school was like. She wanted to experience what being a normal child was like.

"Alright, that's settled. I will get our Xiuying enrolled tomorrow, first thing in the morning," Yilin declared.

Meili suddenly rushed through the front door and stomped her feet on the floor.

"I am *never* going back to that place!" she screamed and plopped herself onto the couch right beside Xiuying with her arms crossed in protest. "They *never* treat me right. Mr. Zen doesn't understand that I'm trying my best, and he keeps pointing out my mistakes." She started to stuff her mouth with cookies. "Ah, I love these, Hua!" she added with her mouth full.

Yilin spoke up, "You know, Meili, that's what teachers are supposed to do. They help you fix your mistakes so that you can learn."

"Ugh, but it annoys me!"

Hua and Lifen laughed while Xiuying smiled.

"I'm so sorry! Where are my manners?" Meili chuckled and went in to hug Xiuying. "It's so great to meet you, finally. I can already tell that we're going to be best friends, just like Hua and my grandmother."

"Me, too," Xiuying whispered, and they started to talk over tea and cookies.

Meili told Xiuying how she loved writing and

wanted to be a writer when she grows up. She had all these imaginations and stories that she couldn't wait to put into words. Xiuying told her how she loved to paint, and she liked to capture moments into pictures so that she could cherish them forever. They clicked instantly, and their friendship began, even though they were different from each other in so many ways. Xiuying was calm and collected while Meili was the definition of *chaotic mess*. Xiuying stayed quiet and kept her feelings to herself while Meili blurted out the first thing that popped into her mind. But together, they were part of one equation, and *that* was the foundation of a strong friendship.

"So, where are your parents, if you don't mind me asking?" Meili asked as they looked toward the fleeting rays of the sun disappearing behind the dreaded mountains.

"They died when I was very young," Xiuying replied.

Xiuying couldn't believe that she had just said that, but she wanted to take Huizhong's advice and start a new chapter in her life. She wasn't going to let her past traumatic experiences define her and speak for her, for who she was. She wanted to do things her way, and she was writing her own story.

"I'm sorry to hear that," Meili replied.

"It's fine. It doesn't really matter anymore. What about your father? Is he around?" Xiuying mumbled.

"He's not around much. You see, our island needs food, wheat that we cannot grow on this soil. He's one of the merchants who arranges all the basic necessities for the village. So, he's traveling almost all the time. He comes home for two days at best after ten days gone." Meili sighed.

"It must be hard; you must miss him."

"Yeah, I do, but at least he's here. The house lights up when he's around. He's caring and compassionate, and he makes up for the times when he's not around. He tries, and that's what matters. So, it's okay." Meili blushed and smiled.

"I admire your spirit," Xiuying praised her.

The sky soon turned purple as the sun was almost gone.

"Ready to go, Xiuying?" Hua asked, and Xiuying nodded.

"See you tomorrow at school?" Meili asked.

"I thought you never wanted to go back," Xiuying replied with a smirk.

"I think I changed my mind." Meili smirked back and waved goodbye.

CHAPTER SIX

"So, how was it?" Hua asked with curiosity as they walked toward their home.

"It was overwhelmingly awesome. I love Meili and her family! I finally have a friend!" Xiuying exclaimed and jumped to show her excitement.

"I knew you'd love them," Hua added.

When they arrived home, Xiuying lit the house with candles while Hua prepared dinner. Xiuying hated the dark, and she insisted on lighting up the entire house. The dark suffocated her. She'd moved on, but the memories were embedded in her mind like a brand.

During dinner, Hua told Xiuying stories of her childhood, how she met her husband, and how they fell in love. They met and instantly connected when she was the only one who could replicate his famous cookie recipe during a competition that he held. They resented each other at first, always in competition, but soon, they fell in love.

Later that night, Hua tucked Xiuying into bed before climbing into her own bed. However, something kept the child awake. She struggled to fall asleep, but she didn't know why. She had a perfect home and the perfect life now, so why was her heart not at peace? The fact that she told Meili that her parents had died was now eating her up. She could have a perfectly normal life, but the memories of her scars were not going away. It wasn't the love for her parents that came back to haunt her. It was the hurt that the love brought, the fear of abandonment, the self-doubt, and the pity.

Xiuying soon found herself struggling to breathe, her own words and thoughts suffocating her. She stepped outside, and the street was empty. The air was foggy, but also so cold that it made her shiver. There were lanterns put on high poles, and Xiuying stood by the Tree of Hope.

"You know, sometimes I wonder how easy it was for people to abandon me, forget about me. I never mattered to anyone I cared about. I've been forgotten, rejected, abandoned. All of my relationships seemed one-sided, my existence unimportant to them. Sometimes it makes me wonder if maybe the problem lies within me. Maybe I'm just not likable," she whispered to the tree and held onto a flower.

Suddenly, her heart started to race again. She could feel her heart beat faster and faster with each passing second. The tingling sensation in her fingers was back, and then she realized that the flower she held was glowing. One after another, all the tiny yellow flowers around her started to glow with a golden light, and specks of dust from them fell onto the ground. The moment the golden dust reached the ground, it started to convert the dry soil into grass, the greenest she'd ever seen.

After a few seconds, the glow from the tree faded, but the grass stayed.

"That's it! That's it!" She beamed and cheered. "I have found my magical power. I can control nature with my emotions. That's what this place needs, greenery! I can't believe this! I can pay Hua back for her taking me in. I can help the island!" Tears of joy started to roll down her face. She looked up at the sky and whispered, "Thank you. The emotions I feel might hurt my soul, but they're going to help others."

She touched the grass, and it felt as soft as wool. She couldn't believe what had happened, as if it was beyond anything she had ever experienced.

Even though she was from a magical kingdom, nobody except Huizhong told her about the powers that she or her ancestors had. Hua believed that things would turn around for this island, and then the universe sent her Xiuying. Xiuying had wanted to help this island, and maybe becoming a tiny speck of hope would help her bring purpose back to her life.

Maybe now, she could justify to herself why she had gone through all the hardships in her life, why she was different, why she understood more than the other children her age. She tucked herself back into bed and closed her eyes. She didn't know how the villagers would react to what had happened when they woke up in the morning, but she was excited to find out.

THE NIGHT FLEW BY IN A BLINK. XIUYING WOKE UP TO VOICES of chatter all around her. It was early in the morning, and the voices felt like a crowd had gathered. She got out of bed and rushed outside. Hua was nowhere to be seen, so she opened the front door to find about forty people gathered around the tree. Hua was standing right in the center of the crowd, and Lifen, Yilin, and Meili were also there. And the head of the village, Jifae, was standing right beside Hua.

"What's happening? Is this a gift from God?" Questions were whispered throughout the crowd.

The island had seen only sand, not even proper soil. It had bushes that were too dry, plants like cacti that one could only find in the depths of a desert, so seeing grass around the tree seemed like a miracle for the villagers.

"Does this mean our island is going to become green again, as mentioned in the myth?" someone from the crowd questioned.

"There, there. Over several decades, our island has been deprived of the gifts that Mother Nature bestowed, but we hoped, and we kept believing. We took care of what was left and saved it from depletion. I believe our time of worry is now over, and Mother Nature is taking back control, just like it should be. This occasion is a cause for celebration, and it should be celebrated. This is just the start. This will create a difference for generations ahead. Don't let your worries take over. Take a deep breath, and let the moment of change sink deeper within your heart," Hua explained, and as she finished, everyone cheered.

The moment felt like a festival. It felt like something that had been yearned for and was now given back to them.

"If this continues, my father would not have to go on those week-long traveling trips. Wouldn't that be great?" Meili exclaimed as she stood beside Xiuying.

Xiuying smiled and looked at her friend, seeing pure joy in her eyes.

"Maybe this is because of you," Meili said, and the words, yet again, made Xiuying's heart race.

"What do you mean?" Xiuying asked, thinking that Meili might have seen her last night.

"I mean, you are the lucky charm," Meili answered and chuckled.

"Oh, I'm sure I'm not. This is all because of the hope the village had. Hua told me all about it," Xiuying answered, trying to remain calm and innocent.

"In light of today's event, I announce a feast of celebration. This day shall be celebrated and remembered," Jifae commanded above them all. "Let the preparations begin; we feast at sunset!" he added, and everyone cheered.

"This is so exciting. Father is also coming back today. This means we have much to do, Xiuying! See you tonight!" Meili waved goodbye and headed toward her own home, accompanied by Lifen and Yilin.

The crowd dispersed within seconds. Everyone had things to do in such a short period of time, and Xiuying was left alone with Hua.

"Oh, Xiuying, my dear. Did you see the miracle? Honey, you brought luck to us!" Hua came over and hugged her.

They walked into their home, and Xiuying felt guilty for not telling Hua the truth. "Hua, I need to confess something," Xiuying muttered.

Hua smiled and sat across from her on a wooden chair. "I know, my dear," she replied.

Xiuying felt confused. "What do you know?"

"Huizhong told me about the magical power you might have because of your family. When you were looking around your new room, he gave tiny glimpses of what you have been through, and I know about the wonderful power that you have within you, my love. Use them for good, and use them wisely," she concluded.

"I'm so glad you know. I didn't know how to tell you," Xiuying said with a sigh of relief.

"I am honored that you wanted to tell me," Hua responded.

"Hua, can we keep this between us for now? I don't have control over my emotions and my power yet. It's all so overwhelming."

"Of course, my dear. It's your life and your decision. My lips are sealed until you want to disclose the gift you have, all on your own. But I hope you do one day. You are a miracle for our village."

"Hua, you are too kind. Thank you," Xiuying replied and beamed.

"Alright, my dear, we have a lot to do! Let's get to work, shall we?" Hua snickered.

"I will start when I understand what's going on. It seems like everyone's in a hurry and has something to do." Xiuying laughed.

"It's been a very long time since we last had a feast of celebration. What happens is that each household has a responsibility. Some bake bread, some prepare the curry, some bake cakes, some bake cookies, some are responsible for the decorations, and some are given the responsibility to entertain. Everyone plays a part that matters, and no one is left behind. Everyone gets dressed up, and we celebrate—

laugh, dance, sing, and eat around the bonfire. It's all in pure joy, my child. It's about spending every moment in gratitude and with the people you love and care about." Hua explained and continued, "So, all you have to do for now is find the prettiest dress in your closet and focus on yourself, whatever you need to do."

"Don't you need help?" Xiuying offered.

"Oh, no. I have been doing this since forever. I can handle it!" Hua replied, and Xiuying went into her room while Hua prepared the dozen cookies that were needed for the feast.

Xiuying's heart felt at peace. There were moments when she felt like her past was taking over her thoughts, but the present pulled her out of despair. She now understood that her power was channeled by her emotions, but was it only from the feelings caused by distress, or could it be channeled by other emotions like happiness, fear, and excitement?

As these thoughts crossed her mind, her hands started to tingle again. She looked around and saw the flowers in her room begin to glow. The specks of dust mixed with the air and escaped through the window, and then suddenly, the grass started to spread faster, around the sides and toward the neighbor's place. A beautiful tree with pure green leaves and tiny pink flowers all over it wrapped the fence on the side of the house.

Xiuying looked out the window and saw only content faces. The villagers were amused, grateful, and now Xiuying felt even more excited because this assured her that the miracle was here to stay.

"So, it *does* work with other emotions!" Xiuying whispered to herself and smiled as she threw on the prettiest dress that she could find in her closet.

THE CELEBRATION WAS ON THE VERGE OF PERFECTION. A cluster of pink flowers had covered some areas of the village, including the center of town where the feast was taking place. The merchants arrived and were shocked. It was hard for them to wrap their heads around what had happened. The entire village was lit with lanterns, colorful flags were displayed all around, the air was mixed with fresh fragrances and delicious aromas, the children were all dressed up, and every woman in town now had a pink flower in their hair. It was as if Xiuying had come to an entirely different place.

Youkai, Meili's father, was the head of the merchants, and they had come back with things needed for the village after a voyage of ten days. They were tired and overworked, but the feeling of helping their own community and bringing them back what they needed kept their minds going even as their bodies were giving up.

Youkai came home and received a heartwarming welcome from his entire family. They, too, were all dressed up and asked Youkai to do the same.

Meili explained to her father everything that had happened. The miracle. Xiuying's arrival.

"So, you think this new girl is the lucky charm?" he questioned suspiciously with a grin.

"I don't think. I *know* she is. And you know what? She's my best friend," Meili replied with enthusiasm.

"Well, I am looking forward to meeting her." Youkai pulled his daughter into a long overdue hug.

Youkai, Yilin, Lifen, and Meili left their home and headed for the center of town. The celebration had already begun, and each family was setting up what they had brought. The bonfire had turned the chilly breeze into warmth.

Hua was already ready and waiting for Xiuying outside her room. The door opened, and Xiuying stepped out. Hua was in awe because Xiuying looked so beautiful. She was wearing a royal pink gown that had bell-shaped sleeves and sparkles all over it. She tied her hair up in a bun and tinted her cheeks a rosy pink.

"You really *are* a princess, my love!" Hua exclaimed, and Xiuying beamed.

This was Xiuying's official public appearance. She was going to introduce herself to everyone as Hua's adopted daughter. As she walked toward the center of Naje, she bit her nails and fidgeted, nervous energy racing through her. She had never been to such a gathering before.

"It's okay, Xiuying. Everyone's going to love you. What's not to love?" Hua comforted her as she held tightly onto her hand and walked to the center of town.

The center was where all the streets met and formed a circle big enough to host a gathering for the entire town. As Xiuying strode in, everyone turned their heads to look at her. She was breathtaking, and her beauty was blinding. The music was loud and getting louder; drums, violins, and guitars all played at once. People were dancing around the bonfire and enjoying the delicious treats that everyone had brought.

"Rumor has it, you're the lucky charm." Jifae came over and greeted Xiuying officially.

Jifae was in his late teens and given the responsibility of the town after his father passed away. He was tall, had black hair, fair skin tone, light blue eyes, and a humble smile. He was known for making wise decisions that benefited the town.

"You and everyone else must be mistaken," Xiuying replied jokingly.

Meili rushed toward Xiuying and gave her a big hug.

"Hello, Gorgeous!" Meili was prone to spontaneous bursts of energy.

"Same to you, Meili." Xiuying complimented her back as she returned the hug.

Xiuying couldn't even finish her conversation with Jifae before Meili dragged her over to the table of freshly-baked buns. Like every other villager, Jifae was also stunned to see the pure beauty of Xiuying. Even

Youkai was delighted to meet her, and he was even happier that Xiuying and Meili were getting along so well.

"I'm predicting that they will become the next Hua and Lifen." He laughed.

The rest of the family laughed alongside him while Xiuying and Meili danced around the bonfire. And for the first time, Xiuying felt loved, seen, and most importantly, she felt happiness like she had never experienced before. She knew she had found her home and her people. She promised herself that she was going to do everything in her power to help them and protect them, forever and always.

CHAPTER SEVEN

TWELVE YEARS HAD PASSED SINCE HUIZHONG LEFT XIUYING at the island, bringing soothing change into her life with the passing of time. She was taller now, had longer hair, and an alluring beauty that drew everyone's attention. However, even her appearance was overshadowed by her irresistible nature and talent. She was known for her forgiving and humble persona, kindness and perfection were her specialty, and her paintings were bought by every household in the village.

Her knowledge had grown with time. She knew everything and had read every book that the village owned, and now with Hua, she, too, advised Jifae with important matters of the village. After all, everyone *did* really believe that she was their lucky charm.

The island was now completely independent. The soil had changed and could now grow all sorts of fruits, vegetables, and wheat. There were grass and trees everywhere, and colorful flowers on every corner of the island. It was safe to say that the island had stopped mourning for the noble warrior and had started to celebrate new life.

Naje was flourishing, but it remained sworn to secrecy. The merchants stopped going on their voyages and started to spend more time maintaining the island itself. It was all working out, socially, economically, and most importantly, environmentally.

And Hua wasn't getting any younger. She was growing weaker with age, but she still had the will to stay active. She and Xiuying bonded over baking her famous cookies, and Xiuying would paint while Hua told her stories about her past.

Lifen passed away peacefully last year, and her death caused Hua great pain. She felt like a part of her soul had been taken away from her. They used to always be inseparable, and now Hua felt like her time to leave was close, too. Hua would often tell Xiuying that after she's gone, everything she had here belonged to Xiuying because her own children never came back to see her.

The thought of losing Hua sank Xiuying's heart. She wasn't ready to deal with yet another loss in her life, and she would always change the topic whenever Hua talked about herself passing onto the next world.

Meili had become a professional writer. She wrote stories for younger children and planned on pursuing a degree in literature in a city an ocean away. Lifen's passing weighed on their family. They missed her, but Youkai's presence made it better. He was now the head of the merchant market, where people traded within the island. Yilin had become a teacher at Meili's old school, and she spent long hours teaching children how to read and write. Meili was still unapologetically cheerful herself, the happy child inside her still alive, but sometimes, the silence inside their home ate Yilin alive. Lifen had taken all the joy with her when she passed.

Xiuying and Meili's friendship had grown stronger as the years went by. They shared secrets, tears, and laughter. They had truly become the next Hua and Lifen, but Xiuying still held secrets of her past that she never shared. She hid them from Meili, just as she hid her magic from the rest of the island. Meili would often ask questions about Xiuying's past, but she never opened up. Instead, she created her own stories and happy versions of her past life, where she talked about Mei as her mother and Huizhong as her father. She would tell Meili stories of how great they were, and the times she'd spent with them.

She was running from her past and using her

imagination and dreams as coping mechanisms. She knew that. Her dreams had gotten to the point where they now felt like true memories that she'd experienced, and she would spend hours upon hours imagining how things would have been if they worked out as they did in her stories. Every time her parents crossed her mind, she would trick herself into thinking that they weren't real. But how long could she continue that? The truth would come for her eventually.

Jifae often visited Hua and had gotten closer to Xiuying. He saw her as a younger sister and valued her opinions and advice.

Xiuying made her way quietly down the hall and knocked on Hua's door one day.

"Hua, can we bake some cookies? You have been in bed for the past two days," she said and sat down beside her. "You are the amazing Hua. Even the walls miss the smell of your cookie dough," she said again, quieter this time.

Hua smiled and held Xiuying's hand. "Xiuying, my dear. I wish I could, but I can't," Hua replied in a faint voice. "I'm afraid I'm much too weak."

Xiuying was worried because Hua's health was depleting day after day, and she feared it would bring a loss that she could never move on from.

"Okay, then. Xiuying, the baker, will be taking over today, and I shall bake the most delicious cookies you have ever tasted. It is *my* time to steal the recipe from *you*, the one you stole from your husband!" Xiuying chuckled at herself.

Hua smiled again and pointed toward her books, letting her know where the recipe was kept.

"Alright, then! Time for me to show what I'm capable of. The best baker on this entire island!" Xiuying claimed and marched toward the kitchen.

"Good luck, my dear," Hua whispered behind her, her voice hoarse.

Xiuying gathered all the ingredients and started to experiment. She didn't know what she was doing, but she was going to at least try. She followed the instructions written and mixed all the ingredients with a keen eye on proportions. She was going to give it her best and do everything she could to make Hua feel better.

Spilled milk, chocolate, and baking powder were sprinkled all over the kitchen counter, but the dough had the same smell as Hua's used to have.

"Yes!" Xiuying danced with joy.

The kitchen was in a state of disastrous chaos, but the cookies came out perfect. She placed the cookie dough in circles on a tray and placed them into the oven for twenty minutes. She had a bit of time on her hands, and instead of cleaning the mess that she had created, she went to check up on Hua.

"Hua!" Xiuying cried in excitement. "You're going to experience the ravishing taste of chocolate chip cookies made by yours truly. This is a once-in-a-lifetime opportunity that you, and only you, will get to enjoy," Xiuying added with a laugh.

Hua drew a light grin onto her face and called

Xiuying over to her side. "Xiuying... thank you," she whispered. "You are the best thing that life has ever given me. I will always be filled with gratitude for the amount of love that you have given me, and for the memories that we have created over the years." Hua's voice suddenly broke as she gasped for air. Xiuying stood still, and tears started to slowly stream down her face. But Hua wasn't done. "Always remember that I love you, and I always will, even when I'm not around, o-okay?" Hua stuttered.

"You don't have to say all this, Hua. I know!" Xiuying sobbed, holding onto Hua's hand.

The silence in the room took over, and then suddenly, the oven timer dinged.

"It's time," Hua whispered again, and Xiuying nodded in tears.

She released Hua's hand and left the room to grab her some cookies, only to come back to a lifeless body.

"Hua?" Xiuying whispered. But when no one responded, she dropped the plate and rushed over, placing her ear over Hua's heart and realizing that she had stopped breathing.

"No!" she cried. "Please, Hua, don't leave me," she sobbed.

The world came crashing down onto her shoulders at that moment. It was an unbearable pain that she couldn't handle. Her body shook, and everything around her swirled.

Hua had died, leaving Xiuying all alone in the home that now belonged to her. The other villagers were saddened by the news, and people started to approach the home to offer their condolences. They considered it to be a great loss for all of Naje, the death of someone whom everyone respected. Xiuying had grown quiet, choosing not to communicate or talk about her feelings to anyone.

The funeral took place at the center of town, the place once celebrated with a large feast and party decorations now covered with flowers of every kind. The entire town gathered there, lit candles for Hua, and said their prayers, wishing her luck in the afterlife.

Xiuying stood by Hua's silent, pale, and lifeless body. Hua was dressed in her wedding gown and had yellow flowers surrounding her. *Sweet*, *kind*, and *considerate* all started to chant in Xiuying's mind and repeated themselves in a loop. She couldn't understand the emotions that she was feeling, and she didn't have time to process any of them before she broke down in front of the entire town. She fell onto her knees, and tears started to drip onto the ground. She had forgotten everything just then, especially the fact that she had magic that was channeled by her emotions. The tears touched the crowd, and all the flowers around her started to glow. The glitter dust fell from them and mixed with the air, traveling to where they were needed.

Everyone witnessed what happened, and they were left in shocked surprise. But in that moment, they understood that it was Xiuying helping their island all along.

The crowd started to whisper, "Is this magic? Did you see that?"

But Jifae interfered. "Alright, everyone! It's time to let Hua go to her resting place."

Xiuying remained frozen on the ground. Meili came to her aid and slowly lifted her up.

"It's time to say your last goodbye," Meili told her, and she looked at Hua one last time.

The villagers buried her in the island's cemetery, and slowly, things returned back to normal, except Xiuying was now seen as a Messiah, a savior. They adored her and worshiped her for her power. But even so, they didn't pester her or ask her to show them more. They knew she was grieving, and they gave her space.

Meili and Jifae took Xiuying home. She sat down in silence and looked around at the mess she had created in the kitchen that morning when she was baking cookies for Hua.

"She didn't even get to taste them," she sniffled.

"Are you okay, Xiuying? We're here for you," Meili said, and Jifae nodded.

Xiuying shook her head but didn't say a word.

The night soon took over, and the clock struck midnight. Jifae left to go home while Meili stayed with Xiuying. She was worried for her friend and didn't want to leave her alone. She joined Xiuying in Hua's room and sat down on the bed with blankets wrapped around them. Meili made a cup of hot cocoa and handed it over to Xiuying. She took it, feeling better than she did before, but was still heartbroken.

"How are you holding up?" Meili asked.

"I don't know," Xiuying replied with a sigh.

"Hey, can I ask you something?" Meili asked, and Xiuying knew what she was going to ask.

"Sure."

"Why didn't you tell me that it was you this whole time? Helping out our island?" Meili paused, took a deep breath, and continued, "That you had a magical power?"

"I never wanted that to define me, and I never wanted you to look at me as a savior or anything." Xiuying started telling her friend how she had gotten her power, and what her life was *really* like before she came to Hua.

"But you left out your whole history. Your family, your rank, your identity—you kept *everything* from me, Xiuying. And here I thought I knew you better than anyone else."

"Not everything. I'm still me. I'm still Xiuying, and I'm still your friend. The only thing that I left out were my... parents."

Meili sighed, defeated. "I can see why you wouldn't want to talk about them. What they did to you was awful and unforgivable."

"Exactly—"

"But," Meili cut her short, "your past is part of who you are today. And after everything we've been through and the life we've made here, you left out that crucial information."

Xiuying's eyes watered. She knew her friend was right, but she couldn't have imagined doing anything different if she had the chance to do it all over. She'd made a fresh, new life with a new family and friends of her own. No matter her parents or her rank, she had been exiled, and her past life ended. She wanted to move forward. But clearly, it had come at a cost.

Meili watched her friend's thoughts race across her expressions. She wanted to be angry, she wanted to stomp her foot and leave, and she wanted time to think this over and ask Xiuying what she was thinking all along. But the tears on her friend's face made her anger melt away. She knew Xiuying hadn't wanted to hurt her. She just wanted a new beginning from her awful past. Meili couldn't forgive her right this second, but she also couldn't stay angry at Xiuying when she had not only lost her past life but had lost Hua, too. She pulled Xiuying into a tight hug and stroked her back.

"It's okay, Xiuying. Thank you for sharing all of this with me," she smiled tightly, whispering into her hair.

Xiuying hesitated at first, but she was quick to hug her friend back. She was thankful beyond belief that Meili had accepted her even after her lies. And even though she knew this wouldn't be the end of this discussion and that this day was going to change everything for her, this hug, this moment with her dearest friend, was enough for now.

Back at the kingdom, things had taken a turn. Qianfan spent the past twelve years pretending to love and protect Xiaofan, all in hopes of bearing a son as his next child. Daiyu was living a blissful life with a perfect daughter and a husband who adored her. She was active in the kingdom, holding galas and listening to the demands and needs of their people. She felt like she was doing it all, being a wonderful mother, a loving wife, and a queen of the people's hearts.

Xiaofan wasn't given the title of a princess, but she was given everything else. She had a room right next to her parents, was treated like royalty, and was sent to the most prestigious school that her parents could find. During her free time as a child, she would spend time with her mother, having tea parties and playing dress-up. She was kind, caring, but a little stubborn, just like her father. Her power was being able to manipulate the wind, for which she was getting trained. She had to learn how to control it and use it in the best way possible.

Even Xiaofan's bond with Qianfan was strong. They played chess together and talked about topics that suited both of their interests. Qianfan hated to admit it, but he also loved his conversations with Xiaofan. Every now and then, he would join Daiyu and

Xiaofan's tea parties as well. He was giving his very best. After all, he knew how to put on a show and fool the audience. Only Qiang could decipher his true intentions.

The past twelve years had been torturous for Huizhong and Mei. Huizhong was considered Qianfan's most loyal soldier, but he was caught handing Xiuying's letter over to Mei, and as his punishment, was thrown into prison for life. On the other hand, Mei, too, was sentenced to life, their prison cells facing each other, and every now and then, they would have meaningful conversations over their experiences with Xiuying. They began to grow fond of each other, and that made their solitary life a little easier. They were being punished for caring, and they were paying the consequence together.

If things had been different, they might have gotten married and had a family of their own. Maybe the imaginary life that Xiuying had wasn't quite far from reality. She was obviously oblivious to what had happened to them, and she often wondered why Huizhong never visited her.

Qianfan had found new ways of torturing them, ways he found enjoyable and pleasurable. He'd starve them of any food or water for days on end. He'd leave them in a cold storage room for hours without any warm clothes. He was eager to punish them, torment them for disobeying him. After all, it was his hatred for Xiuying that brought the worst version of him out.

When she could, Mei always prayed for Xiuying.

That was what kept her going, the will to pray for the girl she'd loved. Daiyu was expecting her third child after twelve years. It was the last month of her pregnancy, and she was already past her due date. This time, she was confident that whatever gender the child might be, it would be loved and accepted.

"It's a boy!" the nurse shouted after ten hours of intensive labor.

Qianfan took a deep breath and sighed with relief. "It's a boy," he repeated, and then chanted again. "It's a boy! We have been blessed with the prince and future king!"

Everyone around them cheered and congratulated Qianfan. He rushed toward the room and grabbed onto his baby boy, cuddling him in his arms. Daiyu's face lit with bliss. She, like Qianfan, also longed to have a son.

"We shall name him Jinhai," Qianfan stated.

"Jinhai," Daiyu repeated and smiled at the newborn.

This time around, the celebration was completely different from when Xiaofan was born. Celebratory galas were going to be held for an entire week. Each household in the kingdom would be sent a box of sweets, and golden coins and free food were to be distributed amongst the less fortunate. Qianfan looked after the preparation himself. Everything had to be *perfect* because, finally, he was blessed with a son.

Xiaofan, staring at all the commotion from a

distance, felt the wind change. Her father suddenly turned his attention from her to her brother, and she couldn't understand why. Daiyu, too, didn't visit Xiaofan for three days after her son was born. She missed them and blamed the birth of her little brother for their lack of attention to her.

The first gala soon began, and piles of presents were brought. Kings and queens from all the other kingdoms came to visit the new prince of Jinu.

"Mother, can I come with you to tonight's gala?" Xiaofan asked.

"Sweetheart, of course you're going to be there, but I will have to stay with your brother. He's going to get marked with the stone today, just like you did," Daiyu answered.

"Were things like this when I was born, Mother?" she asked.

"Of course, how could they not be? You're equally special to us," Daiyu told Xiaofan and hugged her.

The ballroom was decorated with flowers, lit candles, and dark blue silk drapes. There were over a hundred main courses prepared, accompanied by several desserts. Xiaofan wore a light blue gown and was escorted by one of her nannies to the gala.

"It was never like this for your birth, or for your sister's," the nanny whispered.

"My sister?" Xiaofan questioned in shock.

"Yes, your father sent her away many years ago. Her name was Xiuying."

Xiaofan stayed silent, trying to understand the

reason behind her father's decision, and she wanted to comprehend his change in behavior toward her.

At the end of the party, Jinhai was marked with the stone. Everyone in the kingdom praised the prince and the future king of Jinu.

Everyone except Xiaofan. Her mind was cluttered with thoughts. She'd just found out that she has a sister she never knew about. Her parents never mentioned her either, and now she was being neglected for her little brother.

Fuming, she marched up to her parents and asked, "Why didn't you ever tell me that I have a sister?"

"Xiaofan, know your place. And it is not important for you to know," Daiyu replied with such an apathetic tone that Xiaofan was thrown back in shock.

"And why is Jinhai a prince, but I'm not a princess?"

Qianfan walked toward her slowly, his footsteps hitting hard on the floor. "Because he is a boy. He is a boy, and he is superior to you, a girl. There's no such thing as a princess."

Xiaofan stepped back; the rage she saw in her father was different than what she'd been used to.

"Where is Xiuying?" Xiaofan demanded. "I want to meet her."

"She's probably dead by now. I sent her away. Hopefully, for good. She has done *nothing* but destroy our family and hurt your mother," Qianfan answered. "And if you don't agree with the decisions I have made, maybe it is time for you to go, too."

"Sweetheart, just go to your room," Daiyu stepped in. "There's nothing for you to worry about. Don't question your father."

Xiaofan nodded in fear of what her father might do to her and left the room with a broken heart and shattered hope. She was living in a glass castle that was bound to break... by someone she loved.

Two weeks had gone by since Hua passed away, and Xiuying had felt alone ever since. Meili and Jifae would come to visit her every now and then, trying to start up conversations and pretending that things were normal, but they weren't, and Xiuying knew that. The villagers were now treating Xiuying like some sort of miracle maker. They'd greet her and thank her every time she went out, and that aggravated her. Their gestures were sweet, but she didn't think she deserved them.

Meili was trying her best to cheer Xiuying up. She'd bring her food and make her coffee every morning. She was there for Xiuying whenever she needed a shoulder to cry on, and she'd listen to Xiuying tell her stories about Hua, but their relationship began to strain. Xiuying had kept so many secrets from her, and Meili felt like she never really knew who Xiuying was, and she was struggling to understand where she stood in her friend's life.

Jifae, on the other hand, was taking care of all the

finances. All of Hua's assets were given to Xiuying—the house, the bakery, and everything Hua had owned. People around the village would randomly drop by with knitted clothes or gifts, anything they could give to help out. Xiuying was grateful, but she felt like the people of the island thought they owed her something, and she didn't know how she could change that.

Hua's death made her relapse, memories of her old life and past trauma returning. With each day passing by, she was losing more and more of herself but still trying to remain strong. She knew Hua would want her to thrive and not remain stuck in her memories. And so, to save herself from self-destruction, she decided to volunteer at the local school... just to come home and fall apart right after. She was starting to feel hopeless, but one day, she heard a tiny whisper.

You can always write to me, even when I'm not there.

The thought of Mei and Huizhong hadn't crossed her mind for quite some time, but she knew what she needed to do. She sat on her bed and took out a quill to write a letter that she might never send.

Dear Mei,

It's weird how time just stops when you get home after a busy day. You tuck yourself into bed to finally rest, but your thoughts won't let you put yourself at ease. The buzz, the commotion, the worries, the chatter, letting all the memories from the past just pour in. The worst part is, you're there all alone with them, unable to escape.

I've recently lost a loved one to this universe, and now I feel like everything I've ever loved has been taken away from me, but maybe that's just life.

The secret that I'd been hiding my entire life is now out, and I'm trapped in a chamber of reflections. Reflections created by the people around me, and I don't know if they represent the real me or who they want me to be, but that's all I see because maybe, it's easier to believe in what others see in you than what you actually are. What do I represent? Abandonment? Betrayal? Unrequited love? Because if I look within, that's all I find, so maybe it's not that bad to see my reflection through someone else's eye.

Sometimes I feel like I am going insane. I dream about people, things, and situations that never happened. In reality, the people I care about don't return the favor, but they still mean something to me. That's something, right?

These dreams keep me going. They keep me happy. They make me look forward to what's ahead in life. I can't experience happiness in reality, but at least, I can imagine it. It's all a lie, I know. My dreams make me feel like the people present in them and their emotions toward me are real, but they're all figments of my imagination. One day, I'll have to accept them for who they are and not the versions I've created in my mind, just not today. For now, this is my coping mechanism, a subtle escape from the harsh realities of life.

It's all a little too much to take in, isn't it? And the worst part is, I can't say any of this out loud. I don't know who to turn to, even though I have some of the most caring people around me. I'm not able to open up to them because I feel like I've betrayed them somehow by hiding the truth.

Pray it gets better from here.

Yours,

Xiuying

Marking her full name brought her some peace. She had felt a lot of emotions at once, but at least now, she had written them down and turned them into words. She felt a sense of ease as she folded the sheet of paper, almost feeling like Mei had heard what she had written. Then she smiled, the yellow flowers on the Tree of Hope glowing and showering dust, bringing her a sense of relief. Xiuying was alone, but Hua was still looking over her shoulder from another life, and Mei was praying for her, wherever she was. And Meili and Jifae were showing up for her nearly every day, cheering her up.

How could things *not* work out in her favor?

CHAPTER EIGHT

HUA ALWAYS USED TO SAY, "YOUR PAINTINGS WILL HELP YOU express more of who you are, and your ideas, values, and morals in a better way. Don't let the artist in you die," and Xiuying remembered.

It had been a month since she stopped painting, and now was the time to get back to it. It was early morning and a rather rainy one. Dark clouds had loomed over Naje, and they were pouring rain nonstop. Meili had come over to Xiuying's place with a thermos of hot cocoa and some freshly-baked bread.

"Hi, Xiuying. How are you? You're in a better mood today," she said with a sigh of relief.

"Yeah, hey, Meili. I do feel better. Much better. How about you?" Xiuying asked and pulled her into a warm hug.

"Just happy to see you happy!" Meili replied with a smile.

They sat around the coffee table and watched the rain pour.

"It's bad, right?" Meili asked.

"What's bad?"

"What else? The weather!" Meili exclaimed.

"Yeah, I guess it *is* pouring pretty hard." Xiuying then paused for a second. "And that reminds me. I have to apologize. I'm sorry I hid my secret from you. I know you're hurt. You don't have to hide it from me anymore, and I truly regret not telling you sooner. I feel guilty for hurting my best friend. You've always been there for me, regardless of the situation."

Meili was quiet before she cleared her throat. "Thank you, Xiuying. I was disheartened, but our friendship can overcome any obstacle. Besides, you had a valid reason for it. I can't blame you," Meili replied as she looked at her friend with a grin.

"Well, that's settled then," Xiuying agreed and offered Meili some cookies that she had just baked.

"I got accepted into the university I applied for, by the way—the literature program!" Meili suddenly spat out.

"That's so great. Congratulations!" Xiuying

screamed with excitement and pulled her friend in for another hug. "You're finally getting what you have always dreamt of. I'm so proud of you. Your grandmother would've been proud, too. So, what's next?"

"I don't know yet, but I start in a month," Meili said hesitantly.

"You're leaving? Already?"

"Only for a short while! And I'll keep visiting, Xiuying. Naje is my home and always will be."

"Well, then, I guess the question now is, what shall we do until it's time for you to go?" Xiuying asked with a grin.

"Literally everything we can possibly think of. I *can't wait* to start creating memories!" Meili laughed.

"I like the sound of that," Xiuying replied and shoved a warm cookie into her mouth. "I love this, too," she mumbled and held the cookie up.

Their conversation was soon interrupted by cries of help coming from outside, and they rushed out the door. The villagers were bringing in injured people, who were all dressed in military uniform and bleeding.

"What happened? Who are these people?" Meili stammered.

"A ship of a royal kingdom has crashed onto our island. The ship has been badly damaged, the waves are wild out there, several people are injured, and they need our help. We can't leave them out there to die!" one of the villagers answered and rushed back out to grab more.

The rain stopped, and Xiuying and Meili were

standing together beside the Tree of Hope, watching the disaster unfold.

HOURS LATER, THE STORM PASSED, BUT THE AFTERMATH brought a worrisome weather over the villagers. The entire village had come together to aid the injured. Medications and homemade remedies were being collected, the local doctor was working tirelessly, and warm meals were being prepped by several households. There were fifteen soldiers and three maids total, all injured, most with bloody wounds that needed to be stitched up. The incident had warped the village into chaos. All the villagers were in great distress, like their own had gotten hurt. They began praying, concerned, and did everything possible to bring comfort to the ones affected. Jifae had ordered each household to take in one injured person and be responsible for providing them with everything they needed, nurturing them until they got better.

"Is there anything I can do?" Xiuying went up to Jifae.

"No, Xiuying. You just take care of yourself."

"Are you sure?" she asked again, and before he could reply, their conversation was interrupted by a young man.

"Are you Jifae?" the man asked, his voice heavy yet collected.

Xiuying turned around and saw a tall man with

broad shoulders standing behind them. He had dark eyes, long black hair, defined cheekbones, and a sharp jawline. He was wearing a white robe with a golden dragon embroidered on it. As soon as Xiuying saw the dragon on his robe, she realized that he was royalty. Dragon embroidery and dragon-related patterns were *exclusive* to the emperor and the royal families of China.

"Xiuying, meet Prince Zhang Wei from the Baoshu Kingdom. His ship crashed onto our island as he was headed home from a voyage," Jifae introduced.

"Nice to meet you," Xiuying murmured in the lowest tone possible, and then started to walk toward her home without waiting for a reply.

Zhang noticed the woman walking away in distress, like something was clearly bothering her, but he chose to ignore it and continued his conversation with Jifae.

"My kingdom will forever be in your debt. You have helped us during a time when we had lost our hopes of survival. Thank you," Zhang thanked the head of Naje.

"It was our pleasure, Prince Zhang. Our village is all about helping one another. We would have done the same for anyone." Jifae smiled as they walked through the streets of the village, taking it upon himself to show the prince around.

Zhang was among those with only a minor injury. He was amazed by the wholesome ambiance the village had and their will to help. He also noticed how green the village was, with colorful flowers surrounding the small cottages.

"So serene," he whispered. "I wasn't aware that this village existed on the island. We thought it was deserted. To see so much greenery behind the mountains..." Zhang drew out with his hands behind his back.

"It is a miracle. We have kept our island a secret for as long as our history goes back. It saves us from all the politics and power plays, and keeps our community together, strong, and most importantly, happy," Jifae replied.

"The greenery around here is beyond anything I have ever seen. It truly feels like a miracle on a rocky island," Zhang commented.

"Oh, this is all because of Xiuying and her power. She can control nature, and I'm not sure how or why, but she helped our island flourish," Jifae replied.

As soon as Zhang heard about the power, he knew that Xiuying belonged to royalty but was hiding it. He knew that there was only one kingdom in all of China that had control over the four elements, but he chose to keep the information to himself. He was now more intrigued than ever to know about the beautiful woman he had seen earlier and why she had walked away.

Xiuying, on the other hand, felt anxious. The way she felt when she was around the prince, the way she looked at him, as if time had suddenly stopped. She was back at home, but she couldn't stop thinking about him.

"He is royalty, Xiuying," she told herself as she slammed the door to her room shut, and that thought reminded her of how royalty had treated her in the past.

She leaned against the wall and looked across to the window. The yellow tree was shining bright, the brightest she had ever seen. What was she feeling? Was it anger? Confusion? Or something else? She didn't know what it was, but one thing she knew for sure, was that she felt something toward the prince.

Before long, the moon replaced the sun, and it became dark outside when she heard a knock on her door.

"Who is it?" she asked.

"Your favorite person!" Meili sang and entered. "Do you always keep this unlocked?" She plopped herself down onto Xiuying's bed with two cups of hot chamomile tea.

"Only sometimes." Xiuying smirked and grabbed her cup.

"Thankfully, everything went well. All the injured soldiers and maids are treated and resting. And no one is in critical condition." She then hopped up and started pacing back and forth in Xiuying's room.

"That's good, right?" Xiuying asked, but Meili was silent in her pacing. "Um, is everything okay, Meili?"

Meili sighed with a frown. "No," she finally said. "Jifae asked for my hand in marriage."

"That's great!" Xiuying laughed. "Jifae is a wonderful person, and I'm sure he'll treat you right."

Then suddenly, that frown slowly turned into a smile. "I know... because I already said yes!" Meili screamed.

"You tease!" Xiuying threw a pillow over at her, but then hopped up to give her a long hug. "I'm so happy for you. You two are going to be great together!" She looked over at her friend, who was now deep in thought. "What's wrong? Aren't you excited?"

"I am, I am." Meili shook her head. "But we were just children not that long ago. And now I'm getting married? How did life fly by so fast?"

Xiuying shrugged. "I don't know. Sometimes I wonder that myself."

"Hey, Xiuying, did you hear about the prince?" Meili asked. "I met him today, really don't know what to make of him."

Xiuying replied, "Seems like all the women in town are gushing over him."

"I hear he's single, and he's looking for someone to sit beside him when he replaces his father as king." Meili looked at Xiuying, batting her eyes.

"Why are you looking at me?"

"Because! You're both royalty!"

"Not anymore. I left that all behind, and I intend to keep it that way." Xiuying paused and started to light some candles. "And besides, I'm sure he isn't interested in me or our little town. He's privileged, and I know privileged people. They don't care about people like us."

"Well, just think about it. I think you two will make a cute couple!"

"Yeah, yeah, sure." Xiuying followed Meili to the front door as Meili got ready to leave.

"And remember to lock your door! You don't want anyone sneaking in here in the middle of the night!" Meili yelled behind her.

THE NEXT MORNING, XIUYING WAS PROVEN WRONG. ZHANG had requested to meet with all the villagers and was interested in getting to know more about their lives. He toured the village alongside Jifae and met with the villagers who were hosting his soldiers.

Within a few hours, the entire village was singing songs of praise. Everywhere Xiuying went—the bakery, the school, and even Meili's home—all she'd hear were compliments to Zhang, how intelligent he was, how charming he was, and how they all wanted to marry him. So much so that she started to grow frustrated and annoyed with the prince, locking herself in her home until they all left. For good.

As Zhang toured the village, all he could think about was getting a chance to see Xiuying again, *the lucky charm* as people called her. His eyes looked around for her, for the beautiful girl he'd met on that very first day, but he couldn't find her. Everyone around him was handing him bouquets of flowers, large and small, to welcome him to Naje, but those flowers only made him think of Xiuying even more.

"I see why you kept this place a secret," Zhang said to Jifae. "It needs to be preserved. The people here and the love they have for each other are rare, and trust me, I've been to many, many places."

Jifae beamed. "Thank you for your kind words and for understanding why things are kept the way they are."

"I assume we have met with everyone on the island?" Zhang questioned in hopes that Jifae would mention Xiuying.

"Yes, I believe you have," Jifae replied, and Zhang's tiny hope began to fade.

"Oh! I almost forgot! You are invited to dinner over at Meili's place tonight. She will soon be my wife, and we would love to have you over, as our gesture of courtesy."

"Of course, Jifae. I would love to attend," Zhang replied.

Zhang and Jifae grew closer and closer with each conversation, almost like they were becoming close friends. He was staying with Jifae for a couple days, and they were beginning to find that they had a lot in common.

On the other side of town, Meili came rushing into Xiuying's home.

"Quick! I need Hua's fruit cake tonight!" she shouted as she slammed the door like she always did, and she took a deep breath before speaking again. "Can you help me make one? Please?!"

Meili continued to plead, getting down on her knees and whispering "say yes" over and over.

Xiuying crossed her arms and stood in front of her friend.

"What's the occasion?" she asked, raising a brow in skepticism.

"Oh, nothing much. Jifae and I invited Prince Zhang over for dinner tonight, to welcome him to our village."

"I hope you know I'm not going," Xiuying stubbornly said.

"Not even for me?" Meili asked. "Not even for your best friend who is leaving in a month?"

"I don't know..."

"Come on! You said we'd make new memories! And this is a new memory!"

Xiuying rolled her eyes and hesitantly agreed, "Fine, but the emotional blackmailing stops here."

"Your wish is my command! See you at eight!" Meili cheered and walked back out the door.

Xiuying groaned as she closed the door behind her, locking it. Even when she tried her best to avoid the prince, it seemed like something was trying to pull them together. The universe, maybe? She thought to herself and scoffed before turning on the oven.

A few hours later, the cake was ready and packaged neatly, her home filled with the delicious aroma that reminded her of Hua.

"What am I going to wear?" she asked herself and walked toward her room. "What do you even wear when you meet a prince?" Her eyes looked around her closet of dresses, rejecting one after another.

She emptied her closet and finally found something that Hua had made for her. It was a long pink robe with ribbons on the sleeves and tiny embroidered white flowers.

"Perfect!" she heard herself say, stopping herself when she realized that she was indeed trying to impress the prince.

She was already drawn to him, whether she liked it or not.

It was nearing eight when she got ready to leave. She slipped on a pair of glass-like heels that Hua had gotten for her from another island when she went traveling, and she undid her hair, letting the long strands flow down her back. She then walked over to her mirror and applied a bit of color onto her lips, and she topped it off by placing a small pink flower in her hair.

"It's not for him; it's for me," she repeated several times and tried to make herself believe in her own words.

The clock soon struck eight, and it was time to leave. She picked up the cake and started to walk toward Meili's house. It was dark now, and the lanterns were lit. The breeze felt chilly, and for the first time in forever, she felt like herself. She felt happy, and deep down, she was eager to meet Prince Zhang.

Xiuying knocked on the door, and when it opened, Meili was standing there, a smile glossed over her face.

"You came!" Meili announced and gave her a kiss on both cheeks.

Xiuying stepped inside and saw everyone seated around the wooden dining table. Meili's home looked unrecognizable. There was a huge vase with flowers and slender candles on beautiful stands that looked like shining stars.

"My dear, you look ravishing!" Yilin greeted as soon as she saw Xiuying.

"Thank you, so do you," Xiuying replied with a smile.

Her eyes moved across the room, and she saw Zhang staring at her. She quickly looked away, but Zhang continued staring. He *couldn't* look away. He almost felt like he never wanted to take his eyes off of her. She looked so beautiful, the vision of perfection. And he suddenly felt speechless.

The feast was soon served. Two roast chickens, pork belly, Yilin's delicious ginseng soup, and the fruit cake that Xiuying had made, served alongside tea and wine.

"Everything looks so good. Thank you for inviting me," Xiuying said as she took a seat at the table... right in front of Zhang.

"Yes, I agree. Meili, you are an amazing host, I must say. You went beyond my expectations," Zhang chimed in.

"Oh, it's nothing. We love a good dinner with our

friends," Meili replied and told everyone to start digging in.

Xiuying didn't say a single word during the entire dinner, focusing on her plate and nodding with a smile every now and then. She could sense Zhang staring at her, and she didn't want to say or do anything that she'd regret.

"Who's ready for cake?" Meili sang as she walked out of the kitchen with a knife. "Xiuying is the *best* baker in this town. Chef's kiss!"

When she served Zhang his piece, he took a large bite and grinned. "This is delicious! I could eat this every day for the rest of my life." He'd hoped that Xiuying would respond to him, but all she did was give him a soft smile. "I'd love to know the recipe and make this myself," he then added.

That did it.

"You bake?" she asked.

"Of course, I do. In fact," he leaned in closer, "I bet I can outbake you any day."

"I'd love to see that," she jabbed at him.

Then he leaned back and chuckled. "Alright, you got me. I don't know the first thing about baking or cooking."

"I figured."

"So, why'd you run away the other day? When we first met?" he asked, taking another bite.

Xiuying shrugged. "I didn't. I just had things to do." She blushed, hoping he wouldn't catch her bluff.

"What a shame. I was going to introduce myself, get to know you a bit."

"Xiuying paints, you know? She's really good," Meili interrupted before turning back to Jifae.

"Really?" Zhang's eyes settled on her again, soft and dancing with his gentle smile. "Well, I'd love to see some of them one day."

"Maybe. Listen, I should really get going. It's getting late, and I have to walk home alone."

"How about I walk with you? It's not safe for a young woman to walk around alone at night," Zhang offered and started to stand up.

And just in time for Meili to step in again. "That's a wonderful idea! You can keep Xiuying safe, Zhang. Let me pack you two some leftovers to take with you."

Xiuying gave Meili a death stare, to which Meili smiled and winked. As much as she tried to stay away from the prince, Meili seemed to be conspiring to bring them together, like some sort of fantasy. And Zhang *definitely* seemed excited, unable to stand still beside her while saying his goodbyes to the rest of the group.

After Xiuying said her own goodbyes, Zhang escorted her out the door. The sky looked like it had stardust sprinkled in it. The moon was in full bloom, casting their shadows on the ground where they walked. The air was chilly but filled with the scent of cherry blossoms.

The silence between them broke when Zhang

asked, "So, why did you *really* run away when we first met?"

Xiuying took a deep breath and replied, "I don't get along with royalty. The first time I met you, I assumed you were just like all the others—privileged and self-centered."

"And now? Do you still think that?"

"No, you're actually quite the opposite." Xiuying shook her head.

"Whew! That's a relief. It means you won't run away the next time I see you, right?" he asked.

"*If* you see me," she corrected him.

"Oh, I'm sure I will. If not, I can *always* find a way." He chuckled.

"Don't you have to go back to your kingdom?" Xiuying asked.

"I do, but I think I'd like to stay here for a few more days, cherish the beauty of this little island a bit more."

When they reached Xiuying's cottage, his fingers briefly touched hers. "You have a beautiful home, just like yourself."

Her cheeks turned a rosy pink. "Thank you, Zhang Wei." She opened her front door and let herself inside. "And thanks for walking me home."

"I'll see you around, Xiuying." He waved as she closed the door behind her.

THE SUN ROSE OVER THE HORIZON, AND SO DID XIUYING. IT was the next morning, and today was her first day teaching at the local school. She looked forward to meeting all the children. She adored children, and she absolutely *loved* teaching. Meili offered to join her. She'd sit in the back of the class, writing her stories, while giving Xiuying emotional support.

Xiuying quickly scarfed down her breakfast of congee with fish and got dressed, putting in extra effort on her appearance. She wore a simple dress with ruffled sleeves and a high neckline, then she tied her hair into a ponytail with a pink floral scarf. Almost everything she had in her wardrobe was related to flowers. Hua loved the fact that Xiuying could control nature, and she always wanted that to be a part of Xiuying's appearance, so Hua made all her clothes with embroidered floral patterns.

Last night's walk hadn't left Xiuying's mind even as she scurried around her house. She had a grin on her face, and it wasn't going away. It was like she had met two completely different people. The Zhang she met on the first day was a prince, someone she hadn't gotten a chance to know, and the Zhang she met last night was charming and friendly, and deeply cared about her village.

There was something different about him. He was royalty and came from a background of privilege, but he seemed so humble, someone who enjoyed going on long walks, someone who liked eating with commoners on simple floor mats, someone who adored the colors of the sky and flowers, someone who appreciated all the little things that people did for him. He thought about others before himself, he was a leader, and he *acted* like one. He was empathetic, his care for his own people not a fabrication, something that was rare for royalty. His aura radiated pure light, and Xiuying knew that she liked him.

She was being drowned by her own thoughts as she started to walk toward Meili's place so they could walk to the school together. She reached out and knocked. Yilin opened the door and welcomed Xiuying with open arms.

"Good morning!" Xiuying cheered.

"Good morning to you, too," Yilin replied as Meili came running out of her room.

"Do you ever walk like a normal person?" Xiuying asked.

"Sometimes, maybe," Meili huffed out of breath. Xiuying chuckled.

As they walked down the streets of the village, Meili spoke up, "You seem happy today."

"Why do you say that like it's a bad thing?" Xiuying asked.

"It's not, but I haven't seen you like this ever since, you know, Hua died."

"I guess I finally feel like myself again. I still miss Hua, but I'm sure she wouldn't want me to be sad all the time."

Meili stopped walking. "Something tells me this is

about more than just Hua." She caught a glimpse of Xiuying's blush. "Is it Zhang? Are you falling for him?!"

Xiuying shrugged. "I don't know. Maybe."

They arrived at the school, and the wooden door creaked open. At first glance, she saw Zhang sitting at one of the desks alongside her students.

"Zhang! What are you doing here?" Xiuying gasped.

He stood up and smiled at her, his pearly whites twinkling under the fluorescent lights. "Just volunteering. Getting to know the children of the village."

"Aren't you just a saint?" Meili laughed.

"Some might say that," Zhang replied, followed by a chuckle.

Xiuying began her lesson on gratitude and hope while everyone listened keenly as she spoke about the importance of showing gratitude toward even the smallest thing. She even told the children about the wonders of Hua and the Tree of Hope.

"It was hope that brought greenery to the island," she said and concluded her lecture.

Following her lesson, she asked the children to write about all the people and things that they were grateful for. And when the children handed in their assignments, so did Zhang. Xiuying looked down at his paper, and he'd written, *I'm grateful for the village's lucky charm.* Xiuying giggled and looked up to see Zhang standing in front of her.

"Care to join me for a walk?"

Xiuying agreed, and then turned toward Meili,

who had her head buried in a pile of books, her hands covered in ink.

"Meili, care to come along?" Xiuying asked.

"Nah, I'm sure you don't want me to." Meili laughed, and then added, "Besides, I have a lot of writing to do. You two have fun! Why don't you show Zhang our spot?" Meili suggested before lowering her head back down.

Zhang and Xiuying quietly walked toward the opposite direction of the village, to the forest that led up a mountain.

"What exactly is *the spot*?" Zhang curiously asked.

"It's just a place a few miles up. You can see the entire village from up there, plus the sunset and the ocean. Meili and I always go there to take a break from the realities of life. She calls it *our spot* because no one else knows about it," Xiuying explained.

"Well, I'm honored that you're taking me there."

They walked through the forest and followed a rocky path to reach the spot. The sun was setting, and the sky was changing colors. It had turned into shades of orange and pink, with a little blue. The ocean was mirroring the sunset, and lanterns were being lit up in the village one by one. The tiny lights were appearing slowly, and the village was covered with flowers from one end to the other.

"This is beautiful, Xiuying," Zhang whispered as they sat on the edge of the cliff, taking in the fading sunset and the twinkle of the village.

"It really is." Xiuying looked at him, admiring the view in front of her eyes.

"This is all because of you. Jifae told me about your magic."

Xiuying stayed quiet when he said that. She didn't know how to respond to something like that.

Zhang continued, "He also mentioned how you helped the village without even letting anyone know about your power. A lot of people wouldn't have remained so silent. You're humble. I like that." Then he turned to her. "So, what's your story? How did someone born into royalty end up on a small island like this?"

"How did you know?" she asked and turned to face him, staring into his eyes.

"Your power. It's pretty obvious that you're from Jinu, the only magical kingdom in all of China."

Xiuying breathed. "I *am* from royalty. My father, Qianfan, sent me away because I wasn't born a boy. He never accepted me, nor did my mother. And according to him, I'm already dead."

"Gosh, I'm so sorry. If I'd known, I wouldn't have pried. Forgive me."

"It's okay. I do feel a little better getting this off my chest. I've been keeping this to myself for years, and it's been such a burden."

"Why don't you just tell everyone the truth so you have someone to talk to?" Zhang asked.

"There are a lot of layers to the truth. The people here love me for who I am, and I don't want them to see me as a walking tragedy. The horrors I'd faced in my past were unlike anything else, and I want to forget about all that, move on." She took a deep breath. "Besides, it doesn't matter if I'm a royal or not. I was abandoned by my family, *forgotten*."

"But that doesn't mean you should just forget about your past. You deserve better than to be treated like a nobody." He leaned over and kissed her on the cheek.

Her heart sank. She felt a tingling feeling inside of her that she didn't know how to explain. Was this love?

The walk back to the village was silent, but Zhang held on tightly to her hand. When they reached her cottage, Zhang told her, "I won't ever let go if you allow me to stand by your side."

Xiuying nodded, and he smiled, giving her another kiss on the cheek before leaving for his own cottage. She opened the door to her home and found Meili sitting in the living room, munching on some leftover cake and sipping a cup of tea that she had just made.

"About time! I've been waiting for you for hours!" she yelled, and then jumped up in excitement.

Xiuying closed the door behind her and walked over to join her friend.

"Have some tea, and then *spill* the tea." Meili laughed and leaned over to hand her a cup. "Come on, say something! What happened with Zhang?"

"We just talked." Xiuying placed her cup of tea on the wooden table in front of her. She wanted to keep all her feelings hidden deep within herself, just as she had with her past all this time. But Meili looked at her with love and hope, and after everything, Xiuying *had* to tell her the truth. "He's so perfect in every way, and I don't know if I deserve to be in his life. Everyone I love seems to always leave me. All I've ever known was unrequited love."

Meili set down her own cup and scooted closer, her voice lowering to a reassuring drawl. "Xiuying, you're overthinking this. He likes you, and it's on *him* if he wants you in his life or not; that's not for you to decide. The only decision that *you* have to make is whether you like *him* or not, whether you want *him* in your life or not. And don't you *dare* say that the only love you have known is unrequited. *I'm* here for you; the *whole town* is here for you. Hua gave you everything, Xiuying." Meili reached out and hugged her. "Let him in your life. I promise you won't regret it."

"You're right; it's time I give myself a chance at love."

CHAPTER NINE

A week had gone by, and Xiuying found herself hanging out with Zhang almost every day, teaching together, baking together. He even kept her company and entertained while she painted. Even the other villagers were growing fond of seeing the two of them together, seeing them as the perfect couple.

And the more time Xiuying spent with Zhang, the more she realized that she was sharing things with him she had never said out loud. In just a few days, he had become someone she could rely on. She told him all about the struggles she'd dealt with as a child, how her parents hated her, how Hua took her in before she died. She even mentioned Mei, Huizhong, her dreams, and the letters.

He knew it all, and most importantly, he understood her. He believed her troubles were all justified, and that she needed to heal, recover from her past trauma. And he promised that he'd help her, bring comfort to her life, and ease her raging thoughts whenever they crept up. The more time she spent with him, the more she found herself letting go of the past.

But the soldiers and maids had now recovered from their injuries, and they were preparing to leave the village soon. After all, Zhang had a life outside of Naje that was unbeknownst to Xiuying.

Jifae and Meili were getting married in just a few short days, the festivities already beginning. And Xiuying wanted to be there for Meili as she picked out her dress, flower bouquets, and wedding cake, but she couldn't stop thinking about Zhang. How he was due to leave the island right after the wedding. She'd gotten so close to him over the past few days, and she didn't want to watch him leave. She couldn't deal with the pain of watching yet another person she loved leave her, abandon her. And even though he was still here with her now, she felt as if her world was already falling apart. What would become of her and Zhang? Did they even have a chance at a future together?

Red roses were scattered everywhere on the day of the wedding. The ceremony was going to take place at the center of town at sunset. Meili was wearing the traditional Chinese wedding dress, a red one, and her face was covered with a matching veil. She looked ravishing, the happiest that Xiuying had ever seen her, and it was showing on her face. Jifae wore a traditional outfit in the same color.

Xiuying wore a magenta silk robe with her hair tied up in a bun, flowers from the golden tree around it. She reached the venue and was left in awe. The entire town had gathered together, holding gifts and presents for the soon-to-be newlywed couple, and Jifae was waiting at the altar. There were numerous lanterns lit, and the walkway down the aisle was covered with red petals, the air fresh and fragrant. The place looked magnificent! And while she was admiring the decorations and ambiance, she felt a tap on her shoulder. She turned around and saw Zhang standing behind her, wearing a white robe with tiny dragon patterns on the sleeves.

"You look beautiful, as always," Zhang whispered, pecking her on the cheek before grabbing her hand and walking with her to their assigned seats.

"You don't look so bad yourself."

Zhang laughed. "I tried my best."

They sat beside each other and waited for Meili to walk down the aisle with her parents.

"Weddings are the best, aren't they? They remind me of how strong love can be, and how important it is," Zhang said, to which Xiuying nodded in agreement. "I've also been thinking about us. I have to leave tomorrow, but I don't want to leave you," Zhang added, looking down at his foot, which was tapping against the ground. "Xiuying, I want you to come with me. There's so much more beyond this place, and I want to live my life with you." He was now looking at Xiuying, hoping for a reply that would make his day. "And I know you have your life here. You're here for a reason, and you've helped this island so much. But think of how many more you can help *outside* of this island. Our kingdom would be honored to have your presence." He paused and held Xiuying's hand. "And I'm not just saying this because I've fallen in love with you. I'm saying this because the talents you have are unbelievable, and you owe it to yourself to share it with the world."

Their conversation was interrupted by Meili's entry, and everyone stood up for her. She walked down the aisle toward Jifae, Youkai holding onto her arm, and Jifae drew tears of happiness while watching his future wife approach him. They stood in front of each other, holding hands and looking into each other's eyes to say their vows.

"I promise to keep you happy in times of sickness and health. I promise to wipe your tears away every time they meet your eyes. I promise to protect you from every problem that life throws our way. I promise to give all of me to you from this day on. I trust you and appreciate you. I love you, Meili. I always have, and I always will," Jifae concluded as he sniffed and wiped his tears.

Meili looked at him with a sparkle in her eyes and said her part next. "You have helped me understand love in a way that I never understood. You have proven to be by my side always and have helped me shape myself into a version that I can be proud of. When we first met, I never imagined that this day would come, but little did I know, I had fallen for you. You have always looked after this town and its people, but I promise to look after you. I love you, too. I always have, and I always will."

The audience was left in tears, moved by the speeches. It felt like everyone could experience them, understand them. The couple was pronounced husband and wife, and after that, the festivities began. The music played, and traditional Chinese cuisine was offered.

But Zhang was worried that he had said too much to Xiuying earlier, that he might've scared her away by coming on too strong. He feared that she'd turn him away and not want to be with him anymore.

When the night fell, and the party ended, everyone retreated back inside their homes, leaving Zhang and Xiuying all alone. They finally had a chance to talk after hours upon hours of chaos and celebrations. They sat around the bonfire that was still lit in the center of town, and Xiuying snuggled close to him, intertwining her fingers between his. Zhang stayed silent, but he held onto her hand. He hadn't stopped ever since he told her he wouldn't let her go.

"I've fallen in love with you, too," Xiuying whispered quietly. "But this is my home, and I'm not sure if I can leave it."

"I promise you that we'll come back here anytime you want, Xiuying," Zhang assured her. "I want to build a life with you... in my kingdom. We can even open up a gallery to showcase all your paintings, build our legacy. Together."

"I'll sleep on it. Let's talk tomorrow." Then she stood up. "I have to go."

But before she could walk away, she felt a tug on her arm. She turned around and felt Zhang's lips press against hers, sending a shiver of warmth up and down her spine. She didn't know what she was feeling, but she also didn't want it to stop. And Xiuying returned the kiss, allowing Zhang to pull her in even closer.

"I love you, Xiuying. And when I say that, I mean it," he said, pulling slightly away.

"I know, Zhang. I know."

Back home later that night, Xiuying thought about the kiss as she tossed and turned, trying to make herself fall asleep. She was torn between her love for Zhang and her love for Naje.

"How can I leave the home that Hua left me? Raised me in?" she asked herself. "Naje has given me so much. Hua is here, and everything that connects me to her is right here. I can't do it!"

She threw the sheets off herself and got out of bed.

She stood by the door to Hua's room, her things still preserved and organized. Her eyes moved across the room.

"What if I'm not welcomed at Baoshu? Zhang is different, for sure, but there's no guarantee that his family will welcome me. They are royalty, after all."

She stepped inside the room and stood in front of the painted portrait that she had made of Hua. Hua looked so happy, her eyes sparkling like they always did, her smile brighter than the glow of a full moon; the painting felt alive. Xiuying then noticed a little note, written on the right corner of the painting.

Home is where your heart is.

Tears began to roll down her cheeks as she read the sentence that Hua had clearly written. Ever since Hua passed, this place felt a little less like home. Everything that Xiuying had associated with *home* was now gone, only fragments of memories left over. The stakes of leaving this place and starting somewhere new were too high for Xiuying. The thought of not feeling welcomed or accepted made her make a decision that she knew she was going to regret later on. But nonetheless, she was bound to it by fear.

"Zhang has to go without me," she said, looking at Hua's painting, and after a few minutes, she tucked herself into Hua's bed and fell asleep.

Hours later, her sleep was interrupted by loud bangs on the front door. Xiuying's heart started to pound. *I can never catch a break*, she thought to herself as she hurried to open the door.

"Guess what?" Meili bolted in with clouds of exhilaration surrounding her, always interrupting at all the wrong times.

Xiuying felt like her head was throbbing with pain from the lack of sleep, and from the fact that she was debating on walking away from something that felt like a fantasy.

"What?" Xiuying asked, showing no interest whatsoever.

"I'm staying!" Meili yelled.

"Staying? In Naje?"

"Yes! I've decided not to go to university!" Meili announced, leaving Xiuying stunned.

"But you've wanted that for so long. Why are you backing out? Did Jifae tell you not to go?"

"No, no, no," Meili repeated. "He has nothing to do with this. This is *my* decision. My wedding yesterday made me realize that I belong here, that my heart belongs here. Even if I leave, my soul will stay. So, what's the point? I love Jifae and my parents. I can't imagine leaving them." Meili grinned. "This is my *home*, Xiuying. I *have* to stay."

"Are you happy?" Xiuying asked.

"The happiest I've ever been," Meili replied.

A sense of realization suddenly struck Xiuying. Meili was taking a leap of faith and trusting the ones she loved. That's what she needed to do, too.

"I love him," Xiuying whispered. "Zhang. He wants me to go with him," Xiuying continued, looking at Meili for a sign.

Meili turned red with excitement for her friend. "Well, what are you waiting for? Do it! Go with him! You two belong together. And when you love someone, you don't stay an entire ocean away from them."

Maybe Meili was right. Maybe the right decision *was* to leave with Zhang. All Hua ever wanted was for her to live her life to the fullest, to chase after what she loved. And who she loved was *Zhang*.

"So, are you going?" Meili asked.

Xiuying took a steadying breath. "I am."

THE MOMENT ZHANG LEFT XIUYING'S COTTAGE, THE possibility of losing her kept him awake all night. All he could think about was Xiuying's answer and the possibility of her rejecting him.

The next morning after breakfast, he went to go see her, eager for an answer. He knocked on the door, only to find Meili inside.

"Where is Xiuying?" he asked, and Meili pointed him in the direction of Hua's room. "In there," Meili calmly said and left to go home, just in time for her first ever breakfast with Jifae as his wife.

Zhang walked across the living room and knocked on the door.

"Who is it?" He heard on the other side.

"It's me, Xiuying." There was shuffling in the room before the door opened. Xiuying looked up at him with damp eyes. She started to speak, but he shushed her.

"I just want to say something before you make your decision," he said, moving closer to her. "I know this decision is hard for you, to leave your home behind and all the memories that you've made. I know you're afraid because of what you've been through before, but I promise you, my love, that I will *never* let your past repeat itself. I'll protect you, from anything. Always." He paused with a lowered gaze, and held her hands. "We're all searching for someone who grounds us, someone who sees us, someone who is always by our side at the end of the day. *You* are that someone to me, Xiuying, and I don't want to lose you."

Xiuying blushed. Seeing her smile made Zhang feel a little spark of hope.

She finally whispered, "Hua once told me that home is where your heart is, and my heart is with you, Zhang."

"That means you'll come?" Zhang asked as he leaned in to give Xiuying a kiss.

"Yes," she whispered, and just as she did, the flower mural painted on the walls of Hua's room started to glow and shower pink dust that sprinkled over them.

"Wow, that's incredible," Zhang whispered, seeing Xiuying's power for the very first time.

"You better get used to this." And they both started laughing.

Later that night, everyone whom Xiuying loved came over to her home for her farewell dinner. Zhang,

Meili, Yilin, Youkai, and Jifae were all gathered in the kitchen.

"I can't believe this is it. Your last night here," Meili lamented.

"I know," Xiuying replied. "It feels unreal. After living in Naje for so long."

Xiuying had prepared a hefty serving of rice, served with chicken and chestnuts. And for dessert, she made her famous fruit cake. The dinner went by with everyone reminiscing and in tears, sharing memories from when Xiuying first arrived on the island. Yilin and Youkai left after dinner and hugged Xiuying goodbye, promising to see her again in the morning before she left.

Jifae and Zhang also left to go home, leaving Meili and Xiuying alone. Saying goodbye to a best friend wasn't going to be easy for either of them. The house was quiet now, the laughter in the air turned into silence. Meili was throwing sheets onto the furniture to preserve them from dust after Xiuying was long gone, and for once, was—quiet. Xiuying walked over to her, and they sat in front of the fireplace.

"This feels so weird," Meili mumbled. "Just last week, *I* was the one leaving. And now it's you. The universe can be very indecisive sometimes." She scooted over to her friend and squeezed her tight into a hug. "I'll miss you, Xiuying. It feels like I'm losing a sister."

Xiuying took a deep breath, trying to take it all in. "You're not losing me, Meili. I promise I'll come back and visit. You know, I used to think that friendship was all about playdates and sharing secrets, but that changed when I met you. It's as if you are the missing piece of my heart, Meili, like we fit perfectly together. You've always been there for me, even during times of despair, and for that, I'll always remember you. Thank you for always being there for me. And because of that, this has been one of the hardest decisions I've ever had to make." Xiuying cried as she curled up her toes in front of the fireplace.

"Oh, look at you getting all sentimental," Meili remarked as she wiped her own tears away. "I don't think I'll ever find anyone else who can tolerate my constant outbursts." She laughed, and Xiuying joined in.

Silence soon took over again, and the two of them stayed quiet, observing the flames of the burning fire that left a trail of burnt ash behind. The bond they both shared was rare. They were inseparable ever since they were just children, and now they were parting ways as adults.

"I guess it's time for me to go now. Jifae's probably all worried, still waiting up for me." Meili tried to put a smile on her face as she stood up. "See you tomorrow?"

"See you tomorrow," Xiuying answered with her own wobbly smile.

Xiuying looked around the place that she'd called home for the past twelve years after she closed the door behind Meili. It felt so empty, so different. The house didn't even seem alive anymore, with all the furniture covered and wooden boxes packed. She was leaving most of her things behind. The only thing she knew she had to take with her was Hua's book of recipes and the painted portrait of Hua herself. She wanted to keep this place sacred and preserve it for as long as she could.

She toured the rest of the house and stopped by the Golden Tree of Hope, the same tree that had made her power and her identity visible to her, the tree that changed her. She knew that despite whatever life had planned for her, she was *never* going to lose hope. She took a deep breath and sat under the tree with her eyes closed. The tree began to glow, and the flowers showered her with glitter dust. When she opened her eyes again, she saw many more trees, bushes, and flowers surrounding her. Sure, she was leaving Naje, but her presence was going to stick around forever.

THE NEXT MORNING, HER LAST MORNING ON THE ISLAND, SHE threw on a white dress that Hua had made for her. Like every other dress of hers, it had embroidered flower patterns on it. She then threw on a pair of matching slippers and pinned a clip onto the side of her head. She heard the door knock, and she hoped that it was Meili. But when she opened it, she found Zhang and his army of soldiers standing in front of her.

"We are here to get your things, Xiuying. The ship

is being loaded, and we should really get going," Zhang informed her and walked in, only to realize that Xiuying hadn't responded. "Are you okay, my love?"

"Yes, yes, I am. I think I've made my peace," Xiuying assured him and stepped outside. Then she turned around and whispered, "Goodbye, Hua," and she locked the cottage door behind her, holding onto the key tightly.

As she made her way to the cove, she noticed the empty streets. Silence. Not a single villager walked around. Even Meili, who had *promised* to come see her, was absent. She felt betrayed, forgotten, like no one cared that she was leaving, possibly for good.

But when she arrived at the ship, she saw the entire village standing there. Everyone—from her students, to the doctor, to her neighbors—were holding onto bouquets of flowers. Even Meili, who had the biggest smile plastered on her face. Yilin walked up to her and gave her a long hug.

"Don't forget about us," Yilin whispered.

"Never," Xiuying answered as she moved on to Meili, who was already in tears. "Oh, Meili!" Xiuying whimpered. "I promise I'll come visit."

"Take care of yourself," Meili sniffled inaudibly. "And be yourself, okay?"

"I will, I promise. What will I ever do without you?"

As Zhang watched the tears unfold, he felt slightly guilty for being the reason that Xiuying had to leave behind those she loved. He felt like he'd asked her to give up too much, but he also knew that he needed to. He was going to ask for her hand in marriage as soon as they reached the kingdom. He was going to ask her to be his wife.

Xiuying knew she had to trust the uncertainty ahead and hope for the best. On the walk to the ship, she realized how far she had come, how she had met people whom she could finally rely on. And for once, it was *her* choice to leave.

The villagers watched as she stepped on, clapping their hands to wish her the best of luck and waving goodbye as she stood on the deck. And when the ship began to sail, Xiuying rushed to the edge and watched as the people she loved began to shrink, smaller and smaller until they finally disappeared.

Zhang was standing beside her, admiring her for her strength, her beauty, and her love for him.

"How did I get so lucky to meet you?" he asked as they both watched the rushing waves.

Xiuying beamed and leaned her head on his shoulder.

"To new beginnings?" he asked again.

"To new beginnings," she whispered and closed her eyes. She wanted to remember every second of this moment.

Xiuying trusted Zhang, but she still had her doubts about returning to a kingdom and interacting with people from royalty. On the ship, she was already being treated like royalty. Zhang had appointed two maids to cater to her needs, and the cook was instructed to make anything that Xiuying wanted. She was given the biggest room on the ship, with off-white velvet sheets on a king size bed. There were glass vases filled with flowers, and a small wooden table that was accompanied by two chairs. The room smelled of jasmine flowers, and that, Xiuying adored.

But as much as she appreciated the efforts that Zhang was making, she wasn't used to this kind of treatment. And she didn't want to tell him. She didn't want him to think that she didn't want to be with him. She didn't want him to think that she was still afraid.

CHAPTER TEN

TIME WAS RACING AGAINST THE WAVES OF THE OCEAN. Xiuying had seen all shades of blue that had ever existed in the sky, the ocean, and soon, four days had passed with just the blink of an eye. Xiuying spent the journey enjoying all her favorite meals and conversing with Zhang, sharing laughter and moments of sorrow that came from stories about their past. The trip helped Xiuying understand Zhang more. She understood that even though he was royalty, a person who spent his entire life in comfort and with the highest level of prestige, he never let that affect his behavior toward others. He understood that he had a responsibility, that he had to take his father's place on the throne, but he wanted to do it with empathy and by winning hearts.

Xiuying felt her fears beginning to fade, and she was ready to embrace whatever laid ahead because she had Zhang by her side. Zhang, on the other hand, felt like he could tell Xiuying anything. He felt like he could be vulnerable around her, and that's what he cherished. He promised himself to never let her down, to never let anyone question her position, place, or worth in his life. He was ready to tell his family and his kingdom about his future wife.

The ship eventually reached the harbor, and the anchor dropped, followed by a loud bang as it met the edge of the ocean. The wooden crates were gathered and loaded onto horse carriages.

It was a big day, and Xiuying was feeling all levels of nervousness. How could she not? She was about to be introduced to Zhang's *entire kingdom* as his lover, some girl he'd picked up from a stranded island.

How would the kingdom react to the news? What would his family think of me? she thought while she combed through her hair with her fingers and tied it with a pink ribbon. She knew she had to make an impression, and a good one at that.

The door to her room opened with a knock. Xiuying turned to find Zhang standing before her.

"Beautiful, as always," he whispered when he

caught sight of her. "Ready for the big day?" He was wearing the same white dragon robe that he had worn when they first met.

"I think so," Xiuying mumbled. "Do I look okay?"

"Okay?" he repeated. "You look stunning, Xiuying. Don't worry, everyone's going to love you, I promise," he consoled her and leaned in for a kiss. "I love you. Remember that. And they will, too."

Xiuying nodded with a smile and grabbed onto his arm. "I hope so."

When they got up to the deck, Xiuying could see a crowd gathered to welcome him. "Are you sure you want me to accompany you like this?" she asked, having second thoughts about making an appearance in such a spontaneous manner.

"I have never been so sure about anything else in my life. You're here because of me, and I will never forget that. I won't leave you behind," Zhang replied with a meaningful gaze.

There were hundreds of people in the crowd, all there to welcome the prince whom everyone thought had disappeared for good. The soldiers and maids walked out first, and they were showered with flowers and cheers welcoming them back. Zhang made his way off the ship with Xiuying beside him, and the crowd cheered even louder. Their walk from the ship to the carriage was filled with prayers and blessings, and Xiuying felt a little more at ease. He opened the carriage door for her and helped her get in. He then followed suit and sat beside her.

"So?" Zhang looked at her. "What do you think?"

"What do I think?" she repeated. "Baoshu is divine!"

She looked out the window and observed her new kingdom. It was much prettier than she'd imagined. It was decorated with red lanterns and dragon paintings on the walls. There were cherry blossoms everywhere in full bloom. And the streets were lined with trading posts, small eateries, and amazing architecture, exemplifying shades of maroon and beige.

The ride to the castle was tranquil as Xiuying continued to study her new environment, adoring Baoshu. When they reached the castle, the main gates opened, and the carriage traveled along a pristine stream full of water lilies and koi fish before reaching the grand entrance. The castle was huge, larger than the one that Xiuying had grown up in, with temples, galleries, gardens, and even a courtyard. The pointed rooftop was a nice shade of dark green, and the main corridors were a combination of white and maroon. Behind the castle were tall and rugged mountains covered with greenery. It all felt so real, yet Xiuying felt like she was dreaming.

Zhang's family was enthusiastically waiting to see him, and they were all standing by opened doors, ready to welcome him. The wheels of the carriage stopped right in front of the staircase that led to the grand entrance of the castle, all eyes on the carriage as the door opened. Zhang stepped out first, and he held the door open for Xiuying. Her heart was now racing faster and increasing with every step she took. She strolled out, and Zhang offered his arm, to which she held onto and beamed.

"It's okay," Zhang whispered to her, and they walked up the steps, soldiers standing on each side with silver swords in their hands.

Zhang's family was looking at them with raised eyebrows as they approached them. Zhang had two sisters—both adopted and from different families who had abandoned their daughters due to the one-child rule—who lived inside the castle. The Baoshu Kingdom was one of the only kingdoms in all of China who defied the one-child rule, refusing to partake in such a horrible tradition. This was also the reason why many other kingdoms hated, yet still respected, them.

Kyrie, the youngest, the light of the castle and adored by everyone, had a fair skin tone, light brown shoulder-length hair, and rich brown eyes. Kamari, older than Kyrie but younger than Zhang, was known for her confidence and strong political opinions. The king would always call her in for consultations. She was taller than Kyrie, had long, straight, dark hair, black eyes, and a complimenting skin tone with reddish cheeks.

The queen of Baoshu, Huiqing, was known for her empathetic nature, which kept her family together. She was shorter than Zhang, had silver strands in her dark braided hair, and a smile that could brighten up anyone's day. The king, Ming, was someone whom people drew inspiration from. He loved his family and prioritized them over everything else. He was tall, had long hair that was always tied in a bun as their tradition preferred, and a muscular figure.

Zhang and Xiuying reached the entrance to see Kyrie running toward them, throwing her arms around her brother.

"Welcome home, Zhang!" she cheered. "I'm so happy to see you! We were all so worried about you!" She grabbed his hand and led him to the front door.

"I'm happy to be home, too," Zhang replied.

"My son!" Ming greeted him in a loud tone.

"You're home!" Huiqing gushed and gave him a hug.

"Glad you're back." Kamari smiled, also leaning in for a light hug.

"Everyone, I'd like you to meet Xiuying," Zhang declared with a spark in his eyes. "We met on the island where the boat was stranded. She's very special to me."

"Oh, really?" Kyrie teased. Kamari giggled.

"Welcome to Baoshu, Xiuying. We're happy to have you here. If you bring Zhang joy, then you bring us joy as well," his mother welcomed her.

"Thank you for having me. I hope I'm not intruding," Xiuying replied with a soft tone.

"Not at all!" Huiqing led them both inside and told her to get settled in the royal wing of the castle, next to Kyrie and Kamari's room.

The two girls showed her the way while Zhang went into his own room, accompanied by his parents.

"Don't worry, you'll see him soon," Kyrie assured her.

"I love your dress. It really suits you," Kamari added as she opened the door to the room. "Here's your room. Dinner is at six!"

"Thank you for escorting me," Xiuying replied, and Kyrie and Kamari left her to gather her thoughts.

Xiuying closed the door and looked around the room. It was so elegant! The walls had drawings of traditional cherry blossom trees, the bed had silk light pink sheets and matching drapes, wooden dragons were carved on all four corners of the room, and the windows opened to a huge balcony that had a view of the entire kingdom. Xiuying took a deep breath and felt a wave of instant relief. Everything was beyond perfect so far. The kingdom was more than welcoming, Zhang's family was already treating her like one of their own. There wasn't a single thing that she could complain about. But still, she feared that it was all too good to be true.

While Xiuying was settling in, Zhang had an earnest conversation with his parents. He sat down with them and told them everything, who Xiuying was, her power, how he'd met her, and how he'd fallen for her. Ming and Huiqing were impressed that their son had found not only a woman of royalty, but a magical one at that.

"I want to marry her," he continued. "I cannot imagine myself with anyone else."

His parents looked at each other, and then his

father replied, "If that's what you want, then you have our blessing, my son." Ming granted his approval, and Huiqing nodded.

She gave Zhang a kiss on his forehead. "Look at you, all grown up and talking about marriage. You've found a lucky one. Love her and cherish her."

DUSK HAD TAKEN OVER THE KINGDOM. LIT RED LANTERNS and tiny oil lamps were placed on every window. Tiny lights twinkling were heard from Xiuying's room, and she woke up from dozing off to find herself still in the room that had appeared in her dream.

"It's real. It's really real," she whispered.

She forced herself to get out from under the comfort of silk sheets on her bed, and browsed her wardrobe to find something suitable to wear to dinner, but she failed to find one that would work.

"What am I going to do?" she asked herself in distress and sat by the window. "If only Hua were here to help me, or Meili to give me advice. I wish you were both here."

She looked out the window and gazed toward the ocean that had almost disappeared into the darkness. Suddenly, the door opened, and two maids came in with a box in their hands.

"A present from Prince Zhang," one of them said, handing the box over to Xiuying and then leaving.

On it was a note saying, *For my one and only, Xiuying.*

Xiuying couldn't help but smile when she opened the box. Inside, was a beautiful magenta gown that had flowers embroidered on it, but with jewels. It was something a princess would wear, but at the same time, it was minimal, something Xiuying could see herself in. She realized that even if Hua and Meili weren't here to look after her, Zhang was here for her, giving her everything she needed. She hadn't seen him since they'd reached the castle. He had responsibilities, things to look after, but Xiuying obviously didn't leave his mind, not even for a second.

She got dressed and looked in the mirror. The Xiuying she saw was much different from the Xiuying she'd been at Naje, but in a good way. She was stepping her way back into royalty, as if the universe was giving her back something that was once stolen from her. She then tied her hair into a low ponytail, dabbed a little blush on her cheeks, and put on some lip balm to match.

Suddenly, there was a knock on the door, and she was surprised to see Zhang on the other side.

"Were you expecting someone else?" Zhang asked as he walked in and sat on a wooden chair that was placed by the window.

"Not at all." Xiuying chuckled and added, "I just didn't know whether I was going to see you before dinner."

Zhang offered her the seat next to him. "I also

thought that, but I couldn't wait any longer to see you, so I came." He paused, and then continued as he held onto her hand. "And there's actually something that I want to ask you. I know this may come as a surprise to you. This might even feel like I'm rushing into it, but I simply cannot wait anymore." Zhang got down onto one knee before her. "Will you give me the honor of being your husband? Will you marry me, Xiuying?"

Xiuying knew what was ahead when Zhang held her hand and said that first sentence. She was flattered but also cautious. It was only her first day here, after all.

"I want to, Zhang. And I wouldn't want to be with anyone else, but I don't know if I'm ready yet for something so big. What if your family doesn't like me?"

"They love you already, Xiuying. I talked to them, and this isn't about them. It's about us. And your decision depends on how you feel about me; that's all that matters."

Xiuying's heart thumped. His words made her realize that she was the only one holding herself back, not because of anyone else stopping her.

"Then yes, Zhang. Yes, I will marry you."

Tears of joy began to creep from his eyes, and he picked her up and spun his fiancé around the room before planting a passionate kiss onto her lips.

"But I don't want anyone to make a big fuss about it. Not until I've settled in."

He nodded. "You have no idea how happy you've just made me."

Zhang escorted her into the dining hall. There was a long wooden table on the floor in the center of the room, with handwoven carpets to sit on. The people of the Baoshu Kingdom were humble, not only Zhang, but his entire family kept their lifestyle similar to the common people.

The table was decorated with vases filled with flowers, and mats that were made from bamboo. But even though the setup was down-to-earth, the menu was not. It had all sorts of dishes, some that Xiuying had never even heard of. There was Peking Duck, fried rice, stinky tofu, chow mein, congee, kung pao chicken, and for dessert, a platter of moon cakes. The room was lit with oil lamps and candlesticks, with a scent of cherry blossoms in the air.

Kyrie and Kamari were already in the room when Zhang and Xiuying arrived.

"Oh, look at you two!" Kyrie sang.

"Come sit with us, Xiuying," Kamari invited her.

"We're going to tell you all of Zhang's embarrassing secrets!" Kyrie declared.

"Yeah! You're going to love this," Kamari added, and Xiuying laughed as she sat in between Kyrie and Kamari.

Kyrie started telling stories from their childhood. She told Xiuying how Zhang wanted to become a cobbler when he was younger and had a habit of shining shoes that people were still wearing. Xiuying laughed while Zhang gave Kyrie a death stare. Kamari told stories about how he was too afraid to sleep in his own room alone, even when he was in his late teens; he'd always get his mother to sleep next to him.

"You used to be such a scaredy cat!" Kyrie teased.

"It was just a phase," Zhang retorted, and everyone laughed. "This is supposed to be a family dinner, but apparently, it's turned into a story session at my expense."

Story time was put on hold when the king and queen entered the room, and everyone stood up in respect to welcome them.

Huiqing came over and hugged Xiuying. "You look wonderful!" she complimented.

Ming and Huiqing took their places side-by-side at the center of the table.

"I'm so glad to see all my children together," Ming remarked. "Your disappearance made us very worried, Zhang."

"But I'm here now! So, let's eat. I'm starving!" Zhang exclaimed.

"You're always starving. How do you eat so much?" Kamari asked.

"Seriously!" Kyrie chimed in.

"Okay, girls, let him eat in peace." Huiqing laughed, and they all dug in.

Xiuying was surprised to see the connection that they all had. It was rare and pure, and something that many royals lacked. But the Wei family was different.

"So, Xiuying, Zhang tells me you're a bit of a

painter?" Huiqing asked.

"I'd like to think so," Xiuying answered, nodding her head.

"I'd love to see some of your work," Ming added.

"But... I left all my paintings back at the island."

"We can get you some supplies. Anything you need!" Huiqing insisted.

"I was actually thinking we could set up a gallery for her, showcase her work to all of Baoshu," Zhang suggested.

"That's perfect! I can help you!" Kamari offered her hand, and Kyrie added, "Me, too!"

Ming intervened, "Will you all please let the girl breathe?" Then he turned to Xiuying. "What do you say? Interested?"

They all looked at her, impatiently waiting for an answer. "Of course, that sounds fantastic."

And they all cheered.

When dinner ended, and it was time for bed, Huiqing pulled her son aside. "Remember, Zhang. You must keep your distance from Xiuying until *after* you are married. It's tradition. An honor of respect."

"That's not fair!" Zhang protested.

"Everything is fair in love and war!" Kamari called out with a laugh.

Then he turned to Xiuying. "Well, I guess I'll have to say goodnight to you here," he whispered to Xiuying and squeezed her hands tight. "I'll see you in the morning?"

"In the morning," she repeated, reassuring herself

yet again that she'd made the right decision moving in with Zhang.

XIUYING WOKE UP THE NEXT MORNING TO THE BIRDS chirping outside her window. The golden light from the sun was coming in through the glass, and the room looked so serene. She got up and realized that the tree in front of her window had suddenly sprouted pink flowers, her emotions causing them to blossom from the immense love and affection that she felt. She exhaled, relieved that Zhang's family knew about her power and still accepted her for it.

But soon, Kamari ruined that peaceful moment by rushing into her room with a platter of food. "Rise and Shine!" she yelled as she came in unannounced.

"Do you ever knock?" Xiuying asked Kamari, reminding her of Meili.

"You should get used to this. I go into everyone's rooms unannounced. That's how I show my love."

Xiuying chuckled. "It's okay. You remind me of a friend I had in Naje who always used to do the same thing."

Kamari smiled. "I'm your friend, too! Let's eat! I want to show you your gallery after."

Xiuying agreed, and they sat together on the balcony with their bowls of congee.

"I love what you did to the tree," Kamari pointed out.

"Honestly, I didn't do anything. It just... happened."

After breakfast, Kamari went to get dressed. She was planning on giving Xiuying a tour of the kingdom before heading over to the gallery. Xiuying was excited to meet the rest of Baoshu. The villagers of Naje had been nothing but kind, and she had no doubt that the people of Baoshu would be the same.

Xiuying, Kamari, and Kyrie soon boarded the carriage and started their journey toward the market square, the busiest area in the entire kingdom. From the sound of it, Xiuying imagined it to be chaotic, but it was quite the opposite. The streets were wide, clean, and decorated with plants, flowers, and artwork. There were also tall poles that held onto large oil lamps lining the streets.

The square was huge and had tons of different shops, with separate streets featuring a different theme—one for clothes, one for produce, one for poultry, one for crafts and handmade décor, and finally, one dedicated solely for artwork.

"This all seems so calm," Xiuying commented as they stepped out of the carriage and walked toward the art.

The gallery designated for Xiuying was located right by the front gate. It looked like her cottage at Naje but smaller, and it had an arched wooden door and a bay window.

"So? How do you like it?" Kamari asked with Kyrie leaning on her shoulder.

"I love it!" Xiuying exclaimed, still in disbelief that she was here at all. This was hers. This was *her* place to make art, showcase it, and show everyone a sliver of herself. Something warm bubbled in her chest, and she couldn't stop her smile from growing.

"Alright, let's get started! I'm a bit of a designer myself," Kyrie claimed. "I can help you set up!"

"And I will go and order some supplies for you, Xiuying. Some furniture, canvases, paints, and wooden paintbrushes. Anything else?" Kamari asked.

"Maybe some plants?" Xiuying suggested.

"Oh, how could I forget that? Flower Queen!"

Kyrie and Xiuying spent the entire day setting up the gallery. They painted the walls white, covered them with paintings and posters, and then they arranged for a corner bakery to serve coffee and moon cakes for their customers. They set up wooden tables and some chairs in a corner, placed oil lamps on the tables, and gave the gallery a finished look by hanging plants by the windows.

When the night fell, they headed home. Xiuying looked out at the houses that raced by as their carriage skipped down the streets. She admired a kingdom that was unlike the rest. It was beautiful, welcoming, and peaceful, yes. But it had shown her in such a short time that it actually respected their daughters. Women were celebrated here, and Kyrie and Kamari were given permission to break the barriers of being a royal. In Baoshu, they were respected and honored, but at the same time, treated as normal people.

When they reached the castle, Xiuying walked into her room to find her closet filled with new gowns and robes that Zhang had sent over. And on her bed, was a note. *You're already beautiful, but maybe these will remind you how beautiful you actually are.*

Xiuying beamed. She always did when he went out of his way to make her feel special. Her heart felt at ease, and she knew it belonged to him. She changed into one of the dresses in her closet and went to join the family for dinner. Everyone else was already present and waiting for her. Xiuying apologized and sat next to Zhang, who lightly touched her hand and smiled.

"Xiuying's gallery is all set up and ready to open in just two days," Kyrie told everyone.

"That's wonderful. We'd love to see it," Ming declared, and Huiqing bowed beside him.

"I have to give the credit to Kyrie," Xiuying answered. "Her decorating skills are impeccable."

While Xiuying, Kyrie, and Kamari went to the market, Zhang had been occupied with the merchants and soldiers. He attended training sessions with them and went over the security checks of the kingdom. They took their kingdom's safety very seriously and were always ready to fight back if ever needed. Their kingdom was powerful, even without having any magical powers. They were respected, looked up to, but mostly, envied by many. Zhang briefed his father on the details, and then after dinner, he asked Xiuying to join him for a walk.

He held onto Xiuying's hand as they walked slowly through one of the gardens of the castle.

"I think some of these plants need your magic touch," Zhang said.

"Zhang, I've been thinking a lot about the other day."

"Hm?"

"About agreeing to marry you."

"You're not going back on your word, are you?"

Xiuying shook her head. "No, I've been thinking more about it, and I'm actually really glad that I said yes. And not just because you're a prince. Because the more I spend time with you, the more I never want to leave your side."

Zhang came to a stop and pulled his fiancé closer to him. "I, too, never want to leave your side. You have my heart and forever will."

Against his mother's words, he leaned down and kissed her, his soft hands roaming up her back, his lips kissing her neck and shoulders.

"I am a man of tradition, but sometimes, I wish I weren't." He breathed heavily into her ear before stepping slightly away.

Xiuying blushed, and suddenly, all the flowers around them started to glow, glitter dust falling on them before dispersing into the air.

"There it is!" Zhang exclaimed.

"I CAN'T WAIT. I CAN'T WAIT!" KYRIE JUMPED IN excitement the next morning, ready to start decorating for the wedding.

"There's so much to do! Where do we even start?" Kamari asked.

"The decorations, the color palette, the dress, cake, menu," Kyrie mumbled and yelled at the same time.

"Alright, tone it down, you two!" Huiqing laughed.

"Don't worry, Xiuying. We will handle everything," Ming assured her. Then he turned to his son and continued, "Zhang, remember, you must go and meet the king of Liaoshan as soon as possible. This is something you cannot postpone."

The room fell silent. During Zhang's last voyage, his ship ended up crashing, and everyone feared the same thing happening again.

"Yes, Father. I will leave tomorrow after Xiuying's gallery opening," Zhang calmly replied.

"We can work on the wedding preparations until then!" Kyrie commented to disrupt the silence, and after a while, everyone dispersed.

Xiuying went into her room to finish up the several pieces that she was going to showcase in her gallery tomorrow, but the thought of Zhang leaving for a voyage wouldn't stop bothering her. She took a deep breath and went onto the balcony.

"It's not like he's going away forever," she told herself.

She stared out at the ships that slowly vanished into the depths of the ocean, how tiny they seemed from where she was, but the weight they could carry was incredible. Then she felt a tap on her shoulder and spun around. It was Zhang.

"There's a Japanese phrase that I read before coming to your island. It's called *koi no yokan*, and it's the feeling when you first meet someone and inevitably fall in love with them. Maybe you don't love them right away. But you will." He took a deep breath and looked at her. "I didn't think I'd be standing here with you right now when I first saw you. I thought you were just some girl on a random island. But as I got to know you more, my heart started to open up, and now I can't imagine a life without you."

Xiuying was listening, but continued to watch the ships leave, one after another.

"Even if I am away, my heart will always be here with you," he whispered.

"How do you *always* know the right things to say?" she teased.

He shrugged, a smirk on his lips. "It's a gift, I guess. Anyway, I should let you get some rest. After all, you have a big day tomorrow."

After he left, Xiuying went back to her canvases, her fingers moving the brushes in a circular motion, mixing the paints and her emotions together. She felt joy and sorrow at the same time, and was confused as to which one she should follow.

It was the night before the opening of her gallery, and she struggled to fall asleep. The only thing she knew how to do that would bring peace to her mind was to write. Write to one of her loved ones whom she could no longer talk to. She had talked herself out of happiness so many times before, and she feared doing that again. Writing seemed to always clear her mind, so she wouldn't make a decision that she'd regret.

Dear Hua,

I'm the happiest I have ever been, or at least, I'm supposed to be. I have found my significant other, the love of my life. He's everything you would have wanted for me. He listens, makes me feel special, his smile and jokes light up my day, he believes in me, but most importantly, he accepts me for who I am. I finally feel seen. I no longer have to dream or trick my mind into thinking that life is beautiful... because it is.

I'm getting married, Hua, and I have my own gallery, with all my beautiful paintings, but something in my heart fears what's ahead. I have trusted uncertainty for the longest time, but this time, it feels different. It feels like the uncertainty is going to bring back some dark times. The possibility of things not working out is suffocating my happiness. Every time Zhang leaves, I fear for his well-being. Every time I take the next step, I fear I might fall on my face.

I am the happiest I have ever been and surrounded by people who adore me, but I wish you were here. I wish Meili, Huizhong, and Mei were all here.

Your daughter,

Xiuying

CHAPTER ELEVEN

THE NEXT MORNING, XIUYING WOKE UP TO HER ROOM FILLED with all kinds of flowers in different colored vases.

"Surprise!" The door to her room opened with a *bang*, and in rushed Kamari and Kyrie.

"Mother also sends her best wishes. She's going to be there at the opening," Kamari added.

"Do you like our present?" Kyrie asked with excitement.

"Wow, I do, but you didn't have to do all this," Xiuying replied sleepily, barely out of bed, and definitely not dressed and ready to engage with the vivacious sisters.

"Nonsense! Of course, we had to. It's a big day for you, and we *are* your family!" Kyrie exclaimed. "That's what families do. They support each other."

Xiuying felt her heart warm. She thought the flowers were from Zhang, but the fact that Kamari and Kyrie did this made her even happier. Zhang wasn't the only one in the household who cared, and the sisters were quickly becoming irreplaceable in her life.

But her thoughts were cut short when footsteps approached from the hall. Zhang stepped into the doorway, his face bright with shock and a small bouquet of flowers in his hand.

"What's going on here?" he asked, examining the room, which was now filled with a concoction of fragrances from the different flowers, the floor partially covered with colorful fallen petals.

"Nothing, but it looks like we outshined you this time," Kyrie sang while Xiuying and Kamari chuckled.

"You got here too late, I suppose," Kamari teased.

Zhang walked in and handed the bouquet over to Xiuying. "It's not about the quantity; it's about the amount of love put in," Zhang said with a curling smile.

"If that makes you feel better!" Kamari poked. "Denial truly *is* your best friend."

"Alright, alright. This isn't a competition." Xiuying laughed. "But thank you," she added, looking from Zhang over to the girls and back. "I can't tell you how much this all means to me." Her eyes watered before she could stop them. She sniffled, wiping her sleeve across her eyelids to muffle her uncontained happiness.

"Aw, don't cry!" Kyrie wrapped her arms around her.

"It's happy tears," Xiuying whispered as Kamari joined in. The sisters squeezed her tight, and Xiuying couldn't hide her warm smile before looking up to find a similar expression on Zhang's face.

The opening of the gallery was beyond anything that Xiuying had ever expected. The king, queen, Zhang, everyone in Baoshu had showed up to admire the paintings. Within two hours of opening, all her paintings had sold out. Xiuying was introduced by Zhang to everyone who came in, and they all praised her for her artwork. Xiuying made new friends, and people adored her. They all knew about her magical power; everyone in Baoshu, much like the villagers of Naje, knew about her and her ability. They even praised her for being some sort of goddess who had blessed them. But even so, her paintings continued to speak for themselves.

The sun was setting over the horizon, the sky changing colors from blue to orange, and the cold breeze making saying goodbye hard as Zhang prepared to leave for his voyage. All the family members were gathered at the entrance to wish him a safe journey. Xiuying was standing beside Kyrie and Kamari while their parents were talking to Zhang. He was wearing his army's royal suit and carrying a mid-sized silver sword.

Xiuying's heart started to thump harder and faster in her chest, her shoulders, her arms, her fingers all tense with anxiety. She wanted to stop Zhang from going on this journey, but how could she do that? How could she stop him from pursuing something that he loved? Especially when he was always her biggest supporter.

He walked up to her and whispered, "I promise, I'm going to return in three days. Remember, you are safeguarding the most precious thing I have or will ever own."

Xiuying's stomach dropped, but she forced herself to nod her head. "Stay safe," she whispered back with a grin.

"Don't worry, she's in good hands," Kyrie assured Zhang as he bid farewell and climbed aboard, followed by a group of soldiers. The group resembled an army to Xiuying. She couldn't shake that image.

The king and queen soon walked away, and Kyrie accompanied them. Xiuying just stood there, watching Zhang's carriage fleet outside the castle doors. The time had come faster than she thought it would. Maybe he really *would* be back before she expected. Maybe.

"He's going to be back in no time, Xiuying. In the meantime, we can continue preparing for the wedding," Kamari said from beside her.

"You're right. I should keep myself occupied,"

Xiuying answered, forcing her fingers to loosen from clenched fists.

"That's the best thing you can do for yourself." Kamari smiled and started to brief Xiuying on the infinite things that they had to do over the next three days. But even with the seemingly endless tasks, Xiuying couldn't seem to shake that tight, uneasy stirring in her stomach.

Over the course of the next few days, Xiuying had much to do, including deciding on a wedding dress, the decorations, the menu, the cake, the flowers—Kamari helped her decide on the hairstyle and jewelry that she would wear. Huiqing also brought some of their family heirlooms for Xiuying to wear and use, as she was going to become the next queen.

The only thing that Xiuying struggled to decide on was the venue. She wanted to wait for Zhang before making that decision. So, in her spare time, she prepared more paintings for her gallery and met with some of the community groups in the kingdom. She was going to donate all the proceeds she made to those in need, as one should. *A true queen at heart*, people would call her.

Finally, on that third day, a day Xiuying thought would never come, Zhang returned home. As his family welcomed him, he walked up to Xiuying and told her to close her eyes.

"Why?" Xiuying laughed.

"Just do it," he answered. She closed her eyes and patiently waited, anxious for what she was going to see when she opened them again. "Okay, you can open your eyes," Zhang whispered. And when Xiuying did, she was shocked to see Meili and Jifae standing in front of her.

"Surprise!!!" Meili yelled at the top of her lungs.

Xiuying jumped and rushed over to hug Meili. "I'm so happy to see you!" she said. "I had no idea when I was going to see your face again."

"Are you kidding? No way was I going to miss your big day!" Meili answered, and Jifae added, "Also, Zhang wanted to surprise you."

Xiuying looked over at Zhang as he beamed at her. "Thank you," she whispered.

But before she could say anything else or fully welcome Zhang home, he was summoned by his father. Meili and Jifae were shown to their guest room and were invited for dinner later with the entire family.

Meili and Xiuying spent the day catching up on what had happened ever since she left the island. Xiuying told her all about Zhang and his family, the kingdom, the gallery opening, and now she felt like her life was complete because everyone who mattered to her was here with her.

"I'm so happy for you, Xiuying. Coming here was the right decision for you. I mean, you're about to become a queen!" Meili exclaimed.

"Just like you're the Queen of Naje."

"You bet I am."

Xiuying brought Meili to her room and showed her the wedding dress and the heirlooms that she had received from Huiqing, and they continued to talk for hours over tea and moon cakes.

Later that night at dinner, they were joined by Kamari and Kyrie, who both befriended Meili quickly. All four of them got along well enough, throwing jokes out, laughing, sharing stories, and teasing each other like they had been close friends all along.

With everyone gathered for dinner, it felt like the place was alive. There were only two days left before the wedding. The preparations were on the verge of completion, and the guests from other kingdoms had started to arrive. For the venue, Zhang and Xiuying decided on the gardens of the castle because they wanted an outdoor wedding, and the gardens were the *perfect* sentimental place. After all, Zhang held the most pleasant of his childhood memories there, and it was also the place where he asked for Xiuying's hand in marriage. There could be no venue *more perfect* for them than the gardens.

Once it was decorated lavishly for the wedding ceremony, Xiuying and Zhang couldn't wait any longer to move forward and spend the rest of their days united together. When the day finally came, they were more than ready.

The entire kingdom was decorated with flowers and lanterns. The gardens were lit up with oil lamps as the sun dipped. The wedding was happening after dusk, there were cherry blossoms everywhere, the decorations were white and pastel pink, there were stick candles on every table, and the menu had more than twenty-five main dishes and ten desserts.

The small list of invited guests soon started to come in and take their places for the intimate ceremony, while the entire kingdom were invited to attend the ball afterward. This created a rumbling wave of talk about the wedding. Gossip and excitement flowed throughout the kingdom. And not only in theirs, but among the citizens of every other kingdom that was invited as well. Soon, the news reached all the way to Jinu, Xiuying's kingdom, one that wasn't invited to the wedding but cared about the news very much. Qianfan and Daiyu were shaken to find out that the prince was marrying the daughter they'd abandoned.

Xiuying walked in, wearing a long and form-fitting cheongsam. It was red with flowers and dragon patterns embroidered on it with silver and gold thread. Meili and Jifae walked Xiuying down to the aisle. She was the prettiest person present, and like always, all eyes were on her. People gasped and sighed contentedly as she slowly walked toward Zhang. He was standing at the front, wearing a long silk white traditional robe that had patterns nearly matching Xiuying's. Even their outfits complimented each other.

As soon as Zhang caught sight of his bride, he could not believe his eyes. How did he get so lucky? To have someone so compassionate, so loving, and so empathetic. Xiuying reached for him, and he held onto her hands with a smile. The ceremony was small, intimate, and was performed in a strictly traditional manner.

After it was over, the *real* celebration began. Zhang and Xiuying were now husband and wife, and while it was their happiness, the entire kingdom celebrated with loud music, fireworks, and firecrackers. Their wedding was like a traditional festival. The ball that was hosted at the castle was divine, and there were kings, queens, princes, and princesses coming up to meet and congratulate the happy couple.

From a distance, Xiuying could see everyone celebrating and dancing in joy—Kyrie, Kamari, Meili, and Jifae. These were *her* people, and this was *her* happy place. A place she could call *home*.

The ceremony ended around midnight, and finally, Zhang and Xiuying got a chance to relax when they got to their new royal suite. It was large—unbelievably *large*. Wardrobes sat at opposite ends of the room, and huge windows lined the walls and opened in one spot to a large balcony that overlooked the entire kingdom. The walls were painted light brown and had paintings of dragons on them, similar to the patterns on their wedding attire. And the oil lamps placed in every corner of the room created slick glowing shadows on the red silk sheets on their bed. This room felt like it was *made* for a king and queen. And now the room—and soon the titles—were theirs.

"I know this is all a little too much, but it's not

going to be like this forever. You can change anything you want," Zhang replied.

"Alright." Xiuying nodded.

"Thank you for letting me be your husband for life," Zhang told her, holding onto her hands.

"And thank *you* for letting me be your wife for life," Xiuying replied, and they both laughed.

"You have never looked prettier. I couldn't even get my eyes off of you," Zhang claimed.

"You didn't look so bad yourself," Xiuying teased.

"Okay? That's all I get?" Zhang laughed. "So unfair," he teased her right back, poking and tickling her as she slid under the silk blankets on the bed.

Xiuying giggled, swatting away his hands before he tucked her in to sleep. He scooted in behind her and pulled her close. She curled into him, soaking in his warmth and reassurances. This would be *their* future. This would be their routine every night. She beamed, warmth spreading through her body until she drifted off to sleep.

Xiuying woke up before Zhang the next morning. Her eyes opened, and she could see his face on the pillow right next to her. His eyes were closed, dreaming of all the things that he wanted to achieve. He held onto her hand even while he was asleep, the golden sunlight touching his face, making the tiny freckles on his cheeks visible. Xiuying got up to push the drapes down so that Zhang didn't get disturbed, when suddenly, she heard a knock on the door.

Who could it be, so early in the morning? she thought.

She opened the door to find a maid standing with a scroll in her hand.

"This came for you in a manner of urgency," she said.

"Is this for Zhang?" Xiuying asked.

"This is for you, my queen," she replied, taking a bow before she turned around and left.

Xiuying held the scroll tightly in her hands. She went to the balcony that faced the kingdom, her heart pounding in her chest. She looked down in her hands and turned the scroll over, and there was the royal seal of... *her family*. A scroll from the parents who abandoned her. A scroll from the father who left her to die. A scroll from the mother who didn't stand up for her own daughter.

Why now? A part of her wanted to throw the scroll away and forget about it forever, but another part of her wanted to rip it open and read what they had to say. It had taken her a decade to forget the memories that caused her pain. Was she going to let them all rush in again? She took a deep breath and gathered her waning courage before tearing the seal apart.

There were two letters inside. One was an invitation, inviting her and Zhang to a royal dinner to strengthen the ties of the two kingdoms. The other was a long note written by Daiyu, addressed only to Xiuying.

Dearest Xiuying,

I know that it has been ages, and you must hate your mother for giving you away and for never being there for the little girl you were. The chains of my marriage and royal responsibilities never allowed me to be the mother you needed, never allowed me to stand up for you, never allowed me to wipe your tears or see you smile. You have fought many battles from a young age, and that, too, was all on your own.

I am sorry, my daughter. I am sorry, Xiuying. I have failed as a mother for both you and your sister. I know there's nothing I can say or do to make you forgive us, but consider the thought of letting your mother see you once more, my daughter. I tried to look for you, but I couldn't find you anywhere. There were no records of you, but you found yourself in royalty once again because that's where you always belonged.

You must be a married woman by the time this letter reaches you. I am sure you must have been the most gorgeous bride that the kingdom has ever seen. Zhang is one of the best in our country, and you are lucky to have each other. I've even heard that you possess one of the rarest powers—emotions that control the environment, and I have never been prouder. I always knew you had something special in you.

Your father asked me to contact you and welcome you back, Xiuying. I hope you find it in your heart to forgive us. I hope your heart is open to letting a little love back in.

Waiting for you,

Your mother and father

Xiuying found herself in rage and tears.

"The audacity!" she screamed.

It was unfair, and she knew they only reached out to her because she was going to become a queen. And the mother of all ironies was that the woman who let her child go—let her die—was now hoping that Xiuying had not turned her heart against them.

How could she? She fell to her knees and started to sob, her eyes turning all red and her body shivering. Zhang woke up to Xiuying crying, and he rushed through the entrance of the grand terrace to find her on the floor.

"Hey, hey, hey," he repeated as he gathered her into his arms. "Xiuying, what happened?" But then his eyes flickered, and he caught sight of the abandoned scroll with her family's seal. He let out a sharp breath.

"It's okay, Xiuying," he whispered. "I am here."

His warmth enveloped her, but her breaths would not slow; her heart would not cease its rampant race. She was choking on her own lack of air. She couldn't get a deep enough breath—she couldn't stop. Zhang repeated his phrase three times before her head grew light, and she collapsed into his arms without even replying. He picked her up and carried her to their bed. He set her atop the blankets and sprinkled a few drops of water onto her face in a rush to make her gain consciousness again. When she jolted awake, he assured her that he was by her side, and she slept unsoundly.

Once Xiuying was asleep, Zhang went back to the balcony and read the scroll that had been sent to Xiuying. His fingers tightened on the parchment paper, tearing a piece off one edge. He understood why the letter bothered her the way it did, and he felt nothing but pure rage and anger for Qianfan and Daiyu. After all, Xiuying had a family now, and a husband who was willing to do and go anywhere to protect her, to make her happy. This was the first time that Xiuying had shed a tear inside their castle, and he *did not* like it.

The day passed by, and everyone in the family soon heard of what had happened. They were concerned for Xiuying more than anything else and wanted to bring her remedies and food that could help with her distress. But when Xiuying awoke again, she only wanted to talk to Zhang.

"I want to visit them," Xiuying whispered as Zhang came over and sat next to her on the bed.

"I don't think you should," he said honestly. "Look at what one letter did to you. Seeing them would only make everything worse, Xiuying," Zhang replied.

"I just want to see their faces. They are blurred fragments in my memory. I know that her letter is not sincere, but she mentioned that I have a sister, and she wronged her. I want to be there for her when no one else has been her whole life. Please, let me do this, Zhang."

Zhang was not fond of the idea, but he knew his new wife was stubborn. He knew the fight in her was far from extinguished. And if she felt that she needed answers and closure for herself and for her sister, then he would be there, too, right by her side.

"Fine. We leave at dawn," he said.

"Thank you," Xiuying whispered.

He smiled and soothed her until she felt ready to face the world again. Meili and Jifae were leaving for Naje the same day, and the goodbye this time was even more distressing than before. Her dearest friends were leaving her side again, and she felt her own limbs being pulled away.

Xiuying cried her heart out later that night, but she put on a brave face in front of her most beloved friends as she watched them depart.

Soon after their friends' departure, Zhang had preparations made for the trip. Three ships were leaving with them—one for themselves, and the other two filled with weapons, soldiers, and presents. They wanted to be prepared for any possible circumstance, and they *never* visited a place empty-handed.

Xiuying and Zhang left, and after a day of traveling through the ocean, they reached the kingdom of Jinu. Their ships were the largest ones on the harbor, earning them even more attention as they exited. Zhang and Xiuying scurried into a carriage that was heavily guarded by ten soldiers. It lurched forward, just as Xiuying's stomach did.

"We can still turn back, Xiuying."

"We have come so far. I cannot just go without knowing about my sister." Xiuying squeezed Zhang's hand.

Zhang had spent the entire day worrying about her

health and had tried his best to make her feel comfortable and happy.

They reached the castle, and all the memories of her leaving rushed back to Xiuying's mind. She had been thrown into a carriage and sent away before, but now the glory she entered in was unmatched and something the kingdom had never seen.

They got out of the carriage after a bumpy ride and were escorted to the grand hall for dinner. It all seemed so dead, so dry, as if the joy from the castle was taken away. Xiuying struggled against the lingering silence, especially after her experiences at her new kingdom.

Footsteps were then heard from a distance, echoing from afar, and after a moment more, Qianfan and Daiyu came into view.

"You came—Oh! My daughter!" Daiyu gushed.

"I am *not* your daughter," Xiuying hissed, clenching her fists. Zhang stood next to her, guarded by soldiers.

"We have brought you gifts," Zhang said evenly, cutting into the tension like a knife.

He asked the maids to bring the gifts in, and they all waited and watched each other as several women scurried in with boxes of fresh fruits, gold coins, and silk cloth. Qianfan was quiet and watchful, but as the final box was set down, Xiuying couldn't hold herself together any longer.

"Where is she?"

"Where is who?" Qianfan raised a brow.

"My sister." Xiuying gritted her teeth.

"What makes you think she's here?" Qianfan laughed. "We sent her to a concentration camp," he declared.

All the blood in Xiuying's veins froze over. All the heat, all the fire, all the fight that had burned brightly inside of her froze over like a pond in the heart of winter.

"What?" Xiuying whispered, but her voice steadily rose. "What did you say?"

Her father smirked.

At the curl of his thin, chalky lips, she exploded.

"How could you?!" she screamed. She turned to her mother.

"Your f-father—" Daiyu stuttered. But Qianfan interrupted her.

"You have no right to speak to her in that tone."

That was when Zhang finally stepped in. "And you certainly cannot talk to Xiuying in *that* tone."

Qianfan glared at him. "Get out."

"Where's Mei?" Xiuying's cries echoed down the empty hall. But she couldn't calm herself; she couldn't lower her volume. Something curled and crawled and wriggled up her throat, threatening to choke her again. "Where's Mei?"

"She's dead!" Qianfan yelled, his voice overpowering hers.

Xiuying stared at him, her eyes wide and disbelieving.

"She died in that bloody prison cell. She never saw

the sunlight after you left the castle." Qianfan sneered, that dark, festering hatred lining every crease, every wrinkle, on his face.

Xiuying shook in her shoes. Her legs wobbled underneath her, and she couldn't... breathe.

Mei had *died.*

Hua had *died.*

Zhang took Xiuying's hand and led her away from the festering dark stares of her parents. Her father watched with that devilish smirk as Zhang pulled her away while her mother dropped her gaze to the floor, unable to meet her eyes. Zhang dragged the shell of Xiuying to the carriage awaiting at the front of the castle, and he whisked her away as quickly as he could.

Xiuying sat quaking in her seat. Once again, she was boarding a ship from the same place, leaving the castle with the same heavy heart. But this time, she *really* had no tie left to her home or to her family. They had taken her—they had taken Mei. And she would *never* see her sister again.

The trip back to Baoshu was silent and tense, but Xiuying barely recognized what was happening. At one point, she was watching the castle gates to her parents' kingdom disappear in the distance, and then the next thing she knew, Zhang was escorting her to their room on the ship. Once she was surrounded by the silence of the cabin, her legs collapsed under her, and her throat let out a muffled cry before she toppled to the floor in a heap.

She woke up again after a few hours and found Zhang waiting by her side. He held her hand firmly in his own, and his foot tapped on the wooden floorboards. She squeezed his hand lightly. Zhang's gaze whirled on her, relieved.

"Hey," Zhang whispered. "We're almost home."

Xiuying sniffled. "I'm sorry, Zhang. You told me not to go, but I did anyway. I should have listened to you."

"It's okay. But you must know, Xiuying, that they don't deserve *anything* from you. Not your attention, not your love, and certainly not the kingdom that they have. I am going to make sure that they pay for how they treated you." Zhang's eyes darkened. A chill rushed across Xiuying's skin, but with it, the fire inside flickered to life.

She went over her father's words again and again and again, but with them, she found herself doubting. When had he *ever* been truthful to her? When had he *ever* respected her or cherished her? Something *wasn't* right, and as much as she wanted to be done with her parents and their delusional games, this one wasn't over yet.

"You're right," she whispered. "They cannot get away with this. And I am going to find my sister and make sure she's okay," Xiuying mumbled.

Zhang looked at her, a thread of doubt passing through his eyes. But he trusted her more than he trusted anyone else. He would follow her to the abyss and back if it meant she would be safe in this life.

“We’ll find her, I promise,” Zhang assured her.

With that, the ship rocked forward, and the voices of the crew called out their arrival. They had returned to their kingdom—their home.

The return home marked a new journey.

A week later, Zhang and Xiuying were crowned king and queen of the Baoshu Kingdom. Immediately, they started making decisions for the betterment of the kingdom, which flourished even more than Zhang’s parents’ era. But not all was bright and cheery for the new royal pair.

Zhang was determined to take over the kingdom that insulted his wife. He wanted to bring Qianfan and his empire to their knees. On the other hand, Xiuying was on a search to find her sister and bring her home. Revenge was all she wanted from the kingdom that she was born into, but she couldn’t achieve that until she had her sister safe and sound at her side once more.

The future was once again unsteady and clouded by fog for Xiuying, but one thing was for certain—Zhang. Their marriage and her love for this kingdom were real. Xiuying was finally safe and had finally found a place and a person to call *home*. Now, she wanted the same for her sister.

To be continued...

ABOUT THE AUTHOR

Viola Tempest is a dystopian fantasy and paranormal romance author who yearns to expose the truth of those in the modern world: the good, the bad, and the ugly. Her inspiration primarily stems from life experiences, those who annoy her, ex-boyfriends, and the crazy dreams that pop into her head every once in a while.

The Forgotten Daughter

THE LOST DAUGHTERS TRILOGY BOOK ONE

VIOLA TEMPEST

www.ingramcontent.com/pod-product-compliance
Lightning Source LLC
Chambersburg PA
CBHW030138010826
48973CB00002B/628

* 9 7 8 1 9 5 9 6 7 1 1 5 2 *